Wanted: Skateboarding Teen

On the freeway, I seriously began to lose it. My brain, my thoughts—they spun wildly in every direction. For the first time in my life, I understood how extreme stress could drive your brain to impossible places. It could warp your thinking, pointing you in dangerous directions, which seemed to make perfect sense at the time.

That's how people kill themselves, I thought. *They get twisted around in their brain.*

I had to calm down. I tried the radio again and tuned in KKNR, the indie-rock station. A commercial was playing: *"I just saved a bunch of money on my car insur—."* I turned it off. I looked at my fists where they gripped the steering wheel. I thought I saw blood on my hands.

That was too much. That was the last straw. I simply could not be doing this: driving like a maniac, losing my mind, swerving through traffic with blood on my hands.

But I was. That was the thing. I *was.*

Other Books by Blake Nelson

THE NEW RULES
OF HIGH SCHOOL
978-0-14-240242-9

ROCK STAR SUPERSTAR
978-0-14-240574-1

PROM ANONYMOUS
978-0-14-240745-5

paranoid park

BLAKE NELSON

speak

An Imprint of Penguin Group (USA) Inc.

SPEAK
Published by the Penguin Group
Penguin Group (USA) Inc., 345 Hudson Street, New York, New York 10014, U.S.A.
Penguin Group (Canada), 90 Eglinton Avenue East, Suite 700,
Toronto, Ontario, Canada M4P 2Y3 (a division of Pearson Penguin Canada Inc.)
Penguin Books Ltd, 80 Strand, London WC2R 0RL, England
Penguin Ireland, 25 St Stephen's Green, Dublin 2, Ireland
(a division of Penguin Books Ltd)
Penguin Group (Australia), 250 Camberwell Road, Camberwell, Victoria 3124, Australia
(a division of Pearson Australia Group Pty Ltd)
Penguin Books India Pvt Ltd, 11 Community Centre,
Panchsheel Park, New Delhi - 110 017, India
Penguin Group (NZ), 67 Apollo Drive, Rosedale, North Shore 0632, New Zealand
(a division of Pearson New Zealand Ltd)
Penguin Books (South Africa) (Pty) Ltd, 24 Sturdee Avenue,
Rosebank, Johannesburg 2196, South Africa

Registered Offices: Penguin Books Ltd, 80 Strand, London WC2R 0RL, England

First published in the United States of America by Viking,
a member of Penguin Group (USA) Inc., 2006
Published by Speak, an imprint of Penguin Group (USA) Inc., 2008

7 9 10 8

THE LIBRARY OF CONGRESS HAS CATALOGED THE VIKING EDITION AS FOLLOWS:
Nelson, Blake, date—
Paranoid Park / by Blake Nelson.
p.   cm.
Summary: A sixteen-year-old Portland, Oregon skateboarder, whose parents are going
through a difficult divorce, is engulfed by guilt and confusion
when he accidentally kills a security guard at a train yard.
ISBN: 0-670-06118-2 (hc)
[1. Guilt—Fiction. 2. Skateboarding—Fiction. 3. Murder—Fiction.
4. Conduct of life—Fiction. 5. High schools—Fiction.
6. Schools—Fiction. 7. Portland (Or.)—Fiction.]
I. Title. PZ7.N4328Par 2006 [Fic]—dc22 2006000277

Speak ISBN 978-0-14-241156-8

Printed in the United States of America
Set in Excelsior
Book design by Nancy Brennan

Thanks: Catherine Frank, Regina Hayes, Nancy Brennan, Sharyn November, Jodi Reamer
at Writers House.

"Young man," he went on, raising his head again, "in your face I seem to read some trouble of mind."

—*Crime and Punishment,*
Fyodor Dostoevsky

FOR DREW

JANUARY 3

SEASIDE, OREGON

(Night)

Dear ____,

I'm here, at my uncle Tommy's beach house. It's about nine o'clock at night. I'm upstairs, by myself. I've got my pen, my spiral notebook. . . .

I don't know how to start. I don't even know if I can do this. But I will try. It can't make anything worse. . . .

Outside it's raining and dark. I can hear the surf crashing in the distance like little bombs going off.

All right. Just went downstairs and made some hot chocolate. *Dude, chill out and write something.* That's me talking to myself. I just have to start at the beginning, take it easy, take it slow. . . .

Paranoid Park. That's where it started. Paranoid Park is a skatepark in downtown Portland. It's under the Eastside Bridge, down by the old warehouses. It's an underground, "street" park, which means there are no rules, nobody owns it, and you don't have to pay to skate. They say some old-school guys built it years ago, and somehow it's survived all this time.

A lot of the best skaters come there, from California and the East Coast and all over. It's also kind of a street-kid hangout. There's all these stories, like how a skinhead got stabbed there once. That's why they call it Paranoid Park. It has that dangerous, sketchy vibe to it.

<hr />

My first connection to Paranoid was through Jared Fitch. He's a senior at my school. He's pretty insane, but cool, though, and one of the best skaters at our school. He does stuff like skating off the back of a delivery truck going forty miles an hour while someone videotapes it.

That's how we became friends. I was just getting good at skateboarding, and he would show me stuff.

He had videos of things he'd done. He also had other skate videos—stuff you couldn't find at the local mall. He just knew what was up, so the two of us became friends.

Last summer we skated every day. We'd go downtown to different places, like this old parking garage that was condemned that everyone snuck into and partied in. That's when we really became friends. And other spots, like the famous "Suicide Stairwell" by the river where everybody used to go. Places like that.

Like I said, I wasn't on Jared's level yet, but I was learning. And he liked that I was young and eager. He liked being the teacher and showing me stuff.

Anyway, during the last week of summer, we were downtown one day and Jared said we should check out Paranoid Park. I didn't say anything at first. I had heard of it, of course, but had never thought of going there. I had assumed it was out of my league. But when I said I didn't think I was ready, Jared laughed and said something like: "Nobody's ever *ready* for Paranoid Park."

So we went. I was nervous, naturally, but I was also kinda psyched. Skating Paranoid. That was an accomplishment. That was something you could tell people about.

We drove over the Eastside Bridge and circled around underneath it. We parked next to an old brick building. I remember seeing train tracks in the street. They were shiny, like they were still in use. As it turned out, they were.

The park itself was above us, tucked right under the bridge. You could hear the cars and trucks rattling by overhead. The area around there was mostly industrial buildings—old warehouses and parking lots, falling-down fences and stuff. There was one real office building farther down the road, so secretaries would drive by every once in a while. They looked a little scared of the kids hanging out there.

We carried our boards up the dirt hill and ducked through a hole in the chain-link fence. We crawled onto the platform and found ourselves looking out over the whole layout. It was actually smaller than I expected, and also kind of trashed. There were old beer cans around, and garbage, and Cholo graffiti. But there was something about it, a kind of aura.

There weren't many people—a couple guys were skating, a dozen or so more stood along the wall to our right. We watched a scrawny older guy in the bowl across from us nail a lip-grind. He wore brown slacks, cut off at the calf, with black socks and black ragged Vans. He had two huge tattoos on his arms and a big scar across his stomach. His deck was some weird old thing, totally beat to hell, but he killed. He was great.

The other guys there were the same. Not only could everyone skate, they all had their own "look." I had seen hard-core skater guys here and there downtown. But I had never seen them all in one place. This was *their* place, I realized. The center of the true skate universe. Or at least that's what it felt like to me.

Jared dropped in and rode up the bowl across from us. I got nervous watching him. Like I said, he was one of the best skaters I knew, but that was nothing compared to those guys. I dropped in, too, and went around a couple times and managed not to make an ass of myself. It was sweet, though—the adrenaline rush of it. You were in the big leagues at Paranoid.

This was the last week of summer vacation. It was also the week Jennifer Hasselbach first called me. She was this girl I'd hooked up with at the beginning of the summer. She had been a camp counselor all July and August, so we hadn't seen each other. But now she was back, and she really wanted to hang out. She called me three times that week.

I wasn't that into it. I mean, she was cute and every-thing. But when I tried to tell her about Paranoid Park, she didn't get it at all. She was like, "Why would you want to hang out at some dirty place if you could go to Skate City?" Skate City was where all the local Preps skated. It was this lame indoor park behind the mall. If she couldn't see the difference, what was the point?

Another thing, and I guess this is important: All that summer, my parents were fighting and talking about separating, so there was a lot of stress about that. My little brother Henry was throwing up all the time. My mom almost moved out, and then she didn't, and then my dad started staying at my uncle Tommy's. It was a bad time; the whole summer was kind of a disaster. I think this was another reason I hung out more with Jared. He was so "out there" that when you were with him, you forgot about everything else. That was also the appeal of a place like Paranoid Park—you got the feeling no matter how bad your family stuff was, those guys had it worse. Those guys were true outcasts. Some of them probably lived their whole lives on the streets. You had nothing on them.

Anyway, so school started. It seemed fun for about a week and then it sucked as usual. Jared and I just got more into skating. We decided to go to Paranoid again. We planned to go on a Saturday night. That Saturday was September seventeenth.

We had it all planned. I told my mom I was going to sleep over at Jared's so we could go early to the Winter Sports Expo. And since Jared's mom was going to Las Vegas that weekend, we would be free to do whatever. We could stay out all night if we wanted.

The only bad thing was that Jennifer Hasselbach wanted me to come out with her that night. She was being really flirty at school, and hinting that she would do stuff. It was tempting. But I really wanted to check out Paranoid. I figured I could hang out with her another time.

So that was the plan. I would get my mom's car. We would stay at Jared's. And we'd go to Paranoid and see what was up.

⬩⬩⬩⬩⬩⬩⬩⬩⬩⬩⬩⬩⬩⬩

But then there was a problem.

All that summer Jared was into this weird college girl, Kelly, who worked at the Coffee People by his house. She was supposedly a sex freak or something, but everyone said she was psycho. Jared had tried to get with her all summer, but it never worked out. But then, that night, she called him from her college. She was bored, and she wanted him to come down to Oregon State and party with her. Needless to say, he said yes.

When I got to his house he was packing for the bus trip. I was so pissed. But there was nothing I could do. Jared figured this was a sure thing, and he wasn't going to pass it up.

I sat on his bed and watched him stuff condoms in his pocket. I said how lame it was that he would blow off Paranoid for some weird girl—especially one who'd denied him all summer. He shook his head. He was sure he would get laid. He said I should call Jennifer. She seemed to want me—what was I waiting for? We could skate next weekend.

But I wasn't that into Jennifer. What I really wanted was to go to Paranoid Park.

<hr/>

I drove Jared to the Greyhound station. He kept talking about how laid he was going to get. I didn't say much. I remember feeling sad when I dropped him off. I remember wishing I had better friends.

That was the thing about my high school. The normal people were boring and the few people that were cool, like Jared, were too crazy. They were fun to hang with, but they could never follow through on anything. You could never count on them.

When I dropped Jared at the bus station he gave me the key to his house, so I could still stay there. The house would be empty, so I still had everything covered. I could call Jennifer or play video games or whatever. I still had the whole night to myself.

I pulled out of the bus station and drove around. For the first time, it felt like fall that night; the air smelled like burnt wood and had that dry foggy taste to it. Other high-school kids were out, driving around; you could feel the excitement in the air of a new school year, new fashions, new music on the radio.

Eventually I got bored of driving. I still had my skateboard in the backseat, and I thought about going to Skate City. But that would suck too much. I thought about checking out Suicide Stairwell but remembered they locked it at night. And they'd fenced off the big parking garage. . . .

Then I pulled a U-turn and drove toward Paranoid Park. I don't know what I was thinking. I wasn't ready to go there by myself. I wasn't good enough. But for some reason, that's what I did.

I circled underneath the Eastside Bridge like Jared had done, but it was so dark and deserted I didn't want to park. I didn't want anything to happen to my mom's car. I drove back over the bridge and parked in the nice part of downtown and then rode my skateboard across.

I found a rusty metal staircase that went down from the bridge. As I walked down, I could see the entire park spread before me. It was crowded on a Saturday night: rad skaters, hot chicks, people partying, goofing around, hanging out. I felt my heart pounding in my chest as I jumped down off the stairs. This wasn't some high-school beer party. This was a serious scene.

I came up with a plan: I wouldn't skate at first, I'd sit and watch and not do anything stupid. Maybe I wouldn't skate at all; maybe I'd just scope things out for when Jared came back.

That's what I did. I found an empty spot along the big cement wall and sat on my board like I was waiting for someone. It totally worked. Nobody bothered me and it was totally fun. I could have sat there all night, watching the skaters and the girls and all the stuff going on. The only bad thing was, I started thinking about other things. Like my parents. My dad had supposedly moved out, but he kept calling the house and bugging us, and my mom was not handling it well. And my poor brother Henry—he was thirteen, and he would get so worried about stuff he'd throw up his dinner. He was like that. He couldn't handle stress at all.

I also thought about Jennifer. She'd seemed pretty determined for us to be together. I mean, she was nice and everything but did I really want to go out with her? Also, she was a virgin, which meant she'd want to "do it" at some point and then things would get all serious. I mean, worse things could happen. I just wished I liked her more. I wished we had more in common—

"Hey," said someone behind me.

I turned around. A creepy guy was sitting on the cement wall above me. He was with another guy and a girl. The two guys stared down at me. The girl lit a cigarette.

"You gonna use that board or you just gonna sit on it all night?"

I shook my head. "Nah, I'm waiting for someone."

"Mind if I use it? While you're waiting?"

"I'd rather not."

"What kind is it?"

I told him. He admitted he didn't know much about

skateboards and asked me about it. I told him what kind of deck it was, what kind of trucks.

He asked to borrow it again. "Just for five minutes. One time around. C'mon. If I don't come back, you can have the girl," he said.

The two guys laughed but the girl didn't. She was younger than them. They had beer and cigarettes and probably other stuff. The two guys were borderline gutter punks. They were dirty and had that hard look about them. Jared called people like that "Streeters."

I didn't want to lend him my board, but I didn't see how I could avoid it. He must have seen this in my face. He hopped down off the wall. "C'mon, bro, five minutes," he said.

"My friend will be here any minute," I said.

"Bro," he said firmly. "Five minutes. And then I give it back. Scout's honor."

I gave it to him.

He looked it over and took it to the lip. A girl on the other side was waiting and he waved for her to go first. He made a big show of it. "No, after you, I *insist*," he told her, waving his hand dramatically. He was kind of a character, I realized. He had a theatrical way about him.

He dropped in. He wasn't technically a great skater. All he could do was ride. But he had style. He wound his way around the park, almost falling several times. Other people laughed when they saw him. "Hey, Scratch!" someone called out. Other people whooped and yelled. He was like the local clown or something. But also, people were a little scared of him, you could tell.

Meanwhile, his friends introduced themselves. I don't remember the guy's name. The girl's name was Paisley. The guy asked me if I came around there often because they had never seen me before. I said just one other time. I remember I didn't really want to look at the guy, but I kind of stared at the girl. She was so young—younger than me, maybe fourteen. Scratch and his friend were both older. The whole situation was pretty sketchy.

"Check out Scratch," said the guy. Scratch had lost his balance and was making a big show of it, waving his arms around, sort of mocking the more serious skaters. He really was like a clown.

After exactly five minutes he came back. He shot up the side of the bowl and caught the board with one hand. He gave it back to me.

"Thanks, friend," he said.

"No problem," I said. I noticed he was missing a bottom tooth, right in the front of his mouth.

Until that moment, I'd been planning my getaway. But once I had my board back I felt safe, or at least safe enough to hang out a little longer. I was curious, I guess, about Scratch and his friends.

We talked. I sat on the wall with them. Scratch and the other guy kept up their banter; they wanted to impress me, I guess. The girl never talked. I kept watching her. She had a homemade tattoo on her wrist and black nail polish and this kind of cave-woman shape to her face. I wondered where she came from, what her family was like, if she even had a family.

Scratch talked the most. He asked me questions about skating stuff, treating me like I was an expert, and always saying how much he loved the philosophy of skateboarding and the rebel nature of it. It was a loner sport, he said. It was like being a samurai but with "boards instead of swords."

I asked him about Paranoid Park, like about the skinhead who got stabbed. He told me the whole story—how the skinhead didn't really get stabbed, and he wasn't really a skinhead, and the whole thing had been wildly exaggerated over the years.

It was fun talking to them. I kept meaning to leave, but I had nowhere else to go, and it was kind of a thrill being there, talking to someone like Scratch. He had lived up and down the West Coast and hopped trains and slept in bus stations and stuff. He said he got in a fight with a cop in San Diego last summer, so he couldn't go there anymore so he was going to crash in Phoenix for the winter and start a band with a friend. It was pretty wild stuff. Especially hopping trains. I always loved trains. I always wanted to hop one.

After a while they ran out of beer. And they needed cigarettes. Scratch said he'd go. Did I have any money?

I figured they would eventually ask for money, so I said I didn't, but then when everyone else had a five, I found a five in my jeans pocket and gave it to them. Scratch asked if I had a car, and I was glad I had left it on the other side of the river. I said I didn't, that I had taken the bus.

Scratch volunteered to walk down the road to a supermarket. It was kind of far, did I want to walk with him?

No. I wanted to hang out. But then the other guy looked at his watch. "Hey the ten-twenty's going to come," he said. "You guys can catch it."

"Hey," Scratch said to me. "Wanna hop a train?"

I looked up at him. I kinda did. "What sort of train?"

"The ten-twenty. It comes right through here every night. We can ride it all the way to Safeway."

They talked me into it. Or I agreed. I don't remember, exactly.

The other guy and the girl offered to watch my board, but I said I would take it with me. Scratch said it would get in the way, but I insisted.

We left Paranoid through the hole in the chain-link fence. I followed Scratch, sliding on my ass down the dirt hill. I watched the back of his stubbly head and hoped I wasn't doing something stupid. He wouldn't rob me, would he? Or take my board? But whatever. I sort of didn't care at that point.

At the bottom of the hill, we dusted ourselves off. That's when I heard the train horn blare. I could feel the rumble of it under my feet.

"That's it!" shouted Scratch, and he broke into an excited run. I ran with him, my whole body tingling with anticipation. I couldn't believe I was doing this. *I was going to hop a train!* Jared would be so jealous. It served him right!

We ran through the old buildings, until we came to the train tracks. The train was really there, it was really coming. The single front headlight shone directly at us.

"Get back," said Scratch when we reached the gravel track bed. "You can't let them see you."

We both ducked behind a loading dock. We crouched there, watching, breathing hard.

The locomotive came even with us. I couldn't believe how big and powerful it looked.

After it passed, Scratch leaned forward. He studied the different cars, watching them pass. Then he picked one and started to jog alongside it.

"Come on, run!" he shouted over the noise.

I clutched my board and dashed after him in the darkness.

The train didn't seem to be going very fast—until you tried to run alongside it. We both had to sprint to keep up. Scratch ran after a metal ladder on the side of a grain car. He jumped for it, caught it, and pulled himself up until he stood on the lowest rung. He pointed for me to do the same.

I still had my skateboard, which was in the way. But I switched it to my left hand and grabbed the ladder on the next car. Still holding my board, I crawled up enough to swing my feet into the bottom rung.

Scratch gave me a thumbs-up when he saw that. I

had proved myself to not be a total idiot.

Now we were on the train. We were riding it. Scratch yelled stuff to me over the noise. He said the train went another quarter mile or so to a train yard. We'd jump off there and walk to Safeway.

I was so psyched. I couldn't believe I was riding a train. I imagined telling all my friends, even telling Jennifer. I secured my skateboard in the rungs of the ladder and hung out as far as I could. Scratch was doing the same. He was a real hobo. The whole thing was so awesome. I wondered if we could ride it the other direction, too. Maybe you could ride it all the way across town.

Unfortunately, after a couple minutes, the train started to slow down. Scratch shouted that we should hop off, the train yard was coming up.

I regretted that my little ride had come to an end. But I had done it. I had hopped a train! I lingered there for a moment, hanging out as far as I could.

Then Scratch began waving frantically at me. I couldn't tell what he was saying. At the same time, he wriggled farther up his ladder and tried to squeeze himself behind it. He looked like he was trying to hide. I didn't understand.

Then I saw the car.

There was a private security car parked on the

gravel up ahead. It faced the train, its headlights shining directly onto the freight cars as they passed. Standing beside it was a man in a security uniform. He had black gloves on and a black nightstick in his hands.

The security guard spotted us immediately. This was my fault. I didn't hide, I just hung there. I didn't know any better.

He ran toward us. He was big, not fat exactly, but he kind of waddled in his security guard uniform. Scratch climbed farther up the metal ladder. He might have yelled something to me, but I didn't hear. I didn't understand anyway. When the security guard reached us, I thought he would yell at us or tell us to get down. I figured we'd hop off and walk away. What could he do to us? Yell at us? Call our parents? There was nothing he could do.

I was wrong. The security guard went for me first. I was high up, so he could only reach my knees. But he took a vicious swing with his nightstick and I swear, if he had connected, he would have broken every bone in my leg. By pure luck and reflexes, I jerked my feet up and he missed. I tried to climb higher, to get away from him. My skateboard almost fell, and I caught it in my chest. The train was still moving, thank God. The security guy had to jog beside it to keep up with us. He took another swing at me, hitting the metal ladder so hard the vibrations nearly shook me loose. I dropped down a rung, almost falling. He wound up to swing again. Now I was vulnerable. I wasn't high enough to avoid the nightstick. And I was losing my grip.

I jumped. I had no choice. I threw myself as far out as I could. I landed hard and tumbled on the gravel. A second later, Scratch jumped, too. The security guard must have tripped or fallen somehow, because when I came out of my roll, he and Scratch were both on the ground.

I scrambled to my feet. I ran for my skateboard. I was going to grab it and run like hell. Obviously, this security guard was out of his mind.

As I snatched up my board, I saw the guard chase down Scratch and hit him in the back with his nightstick. It dropped Scratch like a gunshot. I swear to God, I thought it killed him. And it was so brutal. Why was some rent-a-cop doing this? For riding on a train? It didn't make sense.

Scratch tried to crawl away. The security guard, breathing hard, stood over him. The guard was big and out of shape, but he knew how to swing that stick. He wound up to hit Scratch again.

I couldn't let that happen. Without thinking, I ran at the security guard and rammed the front of my board into his ribs.

He barely noticed. He was very big. But he did turn and swing the club at me, this time just missing my head. I could sense the weight of the stick as it cut through the air above me. It seemed to have metal or lead in it.

Scratch, meanwhile, scrambled to his feet and ran toward the train. The guard caught the back of his shirt for a moment and swung again with his nightstick. By now I was so scared I didn't know what was happening. I honestly thought he was going to kill us both.

So I charged him again. I reared back with my skateboard and slammed it into the back of his fleshy head. I put all my weight into it this time and I could feel the *thock* of my board hitting his skull. He definitely felt it this time. He froze for a moment, then stumbled, then fell forward onto the gravel beside the train.

Scratch and I both ran back a few feet, watching to see if he would get up. He started to—he lifted his head and felt around in the gravel for his nightstick. When he found it he struggled to stand.

Then something strange happened. It was hard to see exactly, in the dark, but it looked like his coat got caught on something under one of the moving cars. It sort of lifted him up and dragged him sideways. Scratch and I were still backing away, but we couldn't resist the bizarre sight of the guard getting pulled along by the train. We watched him try to reach around and unhook himself, all the while skipping sideways, like a crab, trying to keep his feet under him.

Then he got turned around. He got twisted into an awkward position under the train. You could see him start to panic and try to tear himself loose. But he couldn't. The train had him, and it was too powerful.

He got folded up. It was like a rag doll getting folded up and stuffed inside a narrow container. The security guard got rolled up and kind of . . . crushed . . . and ground into a ball.

It must have broken his back. Or his neck. He probably died right then. When the train finally released him—ripping the collar off his coat—it left him sprawled over the track. He lay there, unmoving for a whole second or two. Then the next row of huge steel wheels got to him. They cut him in half. We watched it happen, not thirty feet away. The wheels cut through his stomach and chest so that his legs and waist were on the outside of the tracks, his head and arms were on the inside.

He didn't scream. There was no sound at all, except for the loud metallic groaning of the train. I stood where I was. I couldn't believe my eyes. The train continued to move while I stood trembling with adrenaline and shock. I couldn't believe what I was seeing: a man cut in half. A man, lying in the gravel, in two parts. I simply could not believe it. It was not possible.

Scratch bolted. He sprinted down the gravel track bed, jumped the ditch, and scrambled over the dirt bank. I never saw anyone move so fast in my life. He looked like a rat, clawing his way up the hill and vanishing into the weeds.

I did not run. I stood. I saw my skateboard a few feet away and picked it up. I stared at the dark spot on the ground where the security guard lay. I took a few steps forward. I felt like I should do something, like I should try to help. A terrible sense of dread flooded into my chest.

The last car of the train passed by. There was no caboose at the end, just one final boxcar. I followed that last car forward to where the body was. I couldn't believe my eyes. Right in front of me was a human body cut in half. A human body that had been alive just thirty seconds before.

Blood was everywhere. It was on the silver train

tracks. It was in the gravel under my feet. I stared at the mangled gash where his insides oozed onto the gravel. They steamed in the cool night air.

And the stink of it. When the smell of his insides reached me, I gagged. I almost threw up. I began to retreat, walking backward, but not quite able to pull my eyes away.

I tripped over something and fell. That broke the spell. I looked around. Where was I? What had just happened? Suddenly the air all around me seemed to crackle with bad energy. A low current of fear seemed to jam the circuits in my brain. I felt like I was out of my body, that my body was no longer my own. I felt like every molecule on earth had turned against me.

My lungs wouldn't work. I couldn't breathe. I lowered my head and tried to steady my breathing. I had to call the police. That was the first thing. I had to call someone. Should I yell for help? But I couldn't get any air. And what if Scratch heard me?

I started walking. I came to the security guard's car. It was still idling by the side of the tracks. The driver's side door was open, and the inside light was on. A copy of *Guns & Ammo* magazine hung off the dash.

There must be a radio inside, I thought. I would call the police. I would explain to them what happened. There had been a terrible accident. They needed to come right away. I leaned inside the car to find the radio, but then I found I didn't want to touch anything.

No, I shouldn't touch things. I should be careful about that. Just in case . . . just in case I needed . . . to what?

I stepped back from the car. I had to think about this. What if I got accused of something? It was an accident, but what if the cops didn't see it that way? Or what if it *wasn't* an accident? I did hit him with my skateboard. Was that against the law? Maybe it was self-defense. I didn't know. I had to think. I had to process in my brain just exactly what had happened. *We were on the train. . . . The security guard saw us. . . .*

It was no use. My brain wouldn't work. I could not maintain a single clear thought. Another wave of panic swept through me. My whole body shook violently. I felt something tickling my jaw. I touched my cheek. Tears were pouring down my face.

I backed away from the car. I had to go someplace where I could calm down for a minute and stop freaking out. I walked in one direction, then another. My brain was in chaos, and my body was in total panic. There was a big parking lot across from the tracks. I went toward it. I walked at first, then walked faster, then I started to run. . . .

Dear ____,

So yeah, that's where I found myself. The hardest thing was not to run. I kept starting to run and then stopping myself. I was also hyperventilating. I tried to remember how you stopped that. You were supposed to breathe in a bag or something.

I ended up running toward the river. I jogged halfway across the parking lot before I realized I still had my skateboard. I jumped on it and instantly fell. I scraped my arm pretty bad, but I didn't stop to look. I jumped up and kept going.

At the end of the parking lot, I found an access road that ran parallel to the river. I could see the River Walk, the long bike path that goes by the river. I had skated it many times. But there might be people there, so I stayed away.

I kept to the access road. My brain was still in chaos, but my body had a definite objective: to get as far from those train tracks as I possibly could. That meant going to the left, going south, along the river. Thank God I had my skateboard.

I pushed along the asphalt as fast as I could. The access road was deserted. The parking lots were deserted. I noticed several places I could have stopped and tried to gather my thoughts. But I didn't. I was running now. And once I started, I couldn't stop.

The good news was: I made good time. The access road went from parking lot to parking lot, none of which were in use. I was putting a lot of distance between myself and that train yard. And no one had seen me.

Then, out of nowhere, a car appeared behind me. I didn't have time to hide. I didn't have time to do anything. It sped past me. It was some sort of sports car, music was blaring, it was going too fast—partiers, obviously. I remembered: It was Saturday night.

I kept skating. I went another half mile or so and came to the Hawthorne Bridge. I had to cross the river at some point, to get to my car. The Hawthorne Bridge had a nice wide bicycle/pedestrian walkway. It was probably the best place to cross. It definitely had the most foot traffic. I picked up my skateboard and ran up the stairs.

There was just one problem: There were actual *people* on the Hawthorne Bridge. And cars. And lights. I was not prepared for this somehow, and I almost retreated back down. But no, I had to keep going, I had to cross, I had to look like I belonged there.

I stepped onto the walkway and almost collided with some old guy on a bike. He had to swerve to not hit me. I jumped back, mumbled an apology, avoided meeting his eye.

More carefully now, I started walking. There were lights everywhere, and for the first time I could really see myself. It was shocking how dirty I was. My hands and arms were black with soot. My T-shirt was streaked with thick slashes of grime. It was from the train. The grain car had been covered in a black, oily dust.

I inspected myself further. I found blood on my elbow where I had fallen in the parking lot. Black dust and dirt and possibly more blood covered my shoes and the bottom of my jeans.

I tried to ignore this and act natural and keep moving. Another bike passed me on the left. To my right I could see the river and the whole of downtown Portland sparkling in the night. The beauty of it made my chest hurt.

I walked. Waves of panic kept hitting me. I wanted to run. I wanted to run more than anything. But I couldn't. I had to stay cool. I had to act normal.

Two women came toward me on foot. I took a long breath and tried to stay calm. I was walking too fast, which was suspicious. I tried to slow down. For some reason, I was afraid to use my skateboard. I would normally have skated across the Hawthorne Bridge. Now I thought people would notice me more if I did.

The two women got closer. They wore short skirts, sexy tops. They had probably come from one of the dance clubs on the West Side. It was Saturday night; of course they had. People were out on Saturday night. Downtown would be full of people. Maybe that was a good thing.

But as they approached, I felt utterly conspicuous. I thought my head was going to explode. *Just keep walking,* I told myself. I forced myself to look at the water, to look down at the city. I held my breath . . . and walked . . . and walked. . . .

They passed me. I let out my breath. I heard their voices trail off behind me. *". . . so his friend comes over and wants to buy me a drink. . . ."*

I thought about women like that. Women in their twenties. What if I missed that? What if I got blamed for the security guard and went to prison and never got to hang out with women like that? What if I missed my whole twenties? What if I went to jail for ten years? Or twenty? Or thirty?!

But it was an accident. It was. It wasn't my fault.

Or was it? Had I killed him? Was it me who actually killed him?

And who decided things like that? And how did they decide? Cops and lawyers, they sat around in back rooms and cut deals like on TV. They figured out how long you'd "go away for," and then they went to lunch.

Another bicycle approached me. I tried to take a deep breath. But nothing felt stable in my chest; everything was broken and loose. If the cops found me . . . if someone asked me a question . . . I would crumble. I would disintegrate. I wouldn't be able to lie; I wouldn't be able to do anything. I had to get to my mother's car.

Later, I could talk to someone. Later, I could call people and figure this out. But that was just it. Who would I call? My mother couldn't deal with this. She would totally lose it. So would my dad. Especially now. It would destroy them. It would destroy everything.

"No, Officer, it's like I told you, we just hopped on for a second, just to see what it was like, and then this security guy attacked us, totally out of nowhere. He was trying to kill us, I swear he was. . . ."

And what about college? I had all my college stuff

to deal with. I had to take my SATs. And do my college essays. My father wanted me to go to Gonzaga, where he went. And I had done well on my PSATs, and my mom even thought I should try for Berkeley or someplace like that, somewhere in California. . . .

"No, Officer, I told you, I didn't know the other kid. I just met him five minutes before. Why do you even need a description of him? He didn't do anything. The guard is the one who did something. He attacked us. Go find that nightstick, you'll see for yourself. It had lead in it. Or something. I swear it did. . . ."

I had blown it. That was the truth of the matter. I had blown my whole life. With one wrong move, I had destroyed any chance I had for a normal existence. All the time and effort people had put into me. My teachers, my parents, the lady who taught me how to swim. Whatever I was, whatever I could have been, I had lost it. In one moment, in one instant, I had lost everything I had ever worked for, everything I ever could have been.

"I'm just a frickin' kid for chrissakes! I was scared! What would you do? How am I supposed to know what his problem was? He had a lead bat. He was trying to kill us! Why can't you understand that?"

Another bicycle passed me. I tried to keep my head down. I must have looked guilty as hell. Cars drove by on my left. Some had their stereos cranked. Saturday night. Party time. Where was I going to go? What was I going to do?

I looked at my hands again, quickly, secretly. They were dirty, scraped; one of my fingers was bleeding. I looked at my blackened shirt. There was blood on it, a couple spots down by my belt. *Whose was that?*

Then I looked at my skateboard. It was dirty, too. I looked at the front of it. It was slightly cracked at the very front. Wasn't that old, though? Hadn't I cracked it earlier that summer?

Then I saw the blood. Or something. There was a tiny black spot right where the point had hit the security guard—

I threw it off the bridge. I threw my skateboard over the side of the bridge. I didn't decide to do it; it just happened. I threw my skateboard off the bridge like it was a hot potato, burning my hands. I didn't see it hit the water. I didn't look. I jammed my dirty hands in my pockets and pretended like I had never had a skateboard.

I instantly regretted it. Did anyone see me throw it? Someone on the River Walk? Someone in a car? Would someone think it was something else? A falling person? A baby? A murder weapon?

Why did you do that? I snarled at myself through gritted teeth.

But it was too late now. And losing the board did one positive thing. It changed who I was. I was no longer a skater. Now I was just some dirty kid walking over a bridge.

I reached my mom's car. It was parked on the street, outside a PJ Schmidt's Seafood Restaurant. People in coats and ties stood outside on the sidewalk. A digital clock on a bank down the street said 11:37.

I unlocked the car with the remote. I got inside and started the engine. But no. I had to stop. This was my chance to take a moment, to think for a second, to figure out the best thing to do. Call the police. Call home. Call someone. I thought about my skateboard. How would I explain to the police why I'd thrown it in the river?

But never mind that. I had to tell someone. I should call 911. If I didn't, I would be in worse trouble. That's what they always told you: Tell the truth or things will only get worse. But was that really true? What if it wasn't even your fault? Or what if it was something that couldn't be undone? In that case, it didn't matter if I told or not. Telling someone wasn't going to help the security guard. And think of what it would do to me and my family. Think of what it would do to my brother Henry.

Then, for one second, I saw the security guard in my head. I saw him running sideways like a crab.

I pushed the image out of my mind. I had to think clearly. What would my dad do? What would a normal family do? We could get a lawyer. My parents already had lawyers for their separation. Maybe that was the thing: Get a lawyer first, then call the police. That's what sports people did. And celebrities. And it usually worked. Didn't it?

But none of these issues mattered to my body. My brain could have debates all night long. My body didn't care. My body wanted only one thing: to get the hell out of there.

I shifted the car into drive. I pulled into the street and almost rammed an SUV that had stopped to let some people out. I missed it by inches. A woman, dressed in a low-cut dress, glared at me like, *What's your problem?* I didn't respond. I slowly backed up and tried it again and this time cleared the SUV. Would that woman remember seeing me? Would the people on the bridge remember me? Would the police be asking people?

I pulled up to the light. I could see the poster, a police sketch of my face:

WANTED: SKATEBOARDING TEEN,

BLACK HAIR, BLUE EYES,

DIRTY FROM TRAIN-HOPPING,
LAST SEEN WALKING ACROSS THE HAWTHORNE
BRIDGE ON SATURDAY NIGHT.

They would totally have me. People would remember. Or would they? When the light changed, I eased down on the gas. I turned up the heat in my mother's car. I was freezing; my whole body was shaking. I turned the heat up full blast.

I clicked on the radio. I tuned in KEX 1190 "News Radio All the Time." When they found the body it would be on the news. It would be everywhere. But I couldn't listen to news now. I turned it off. Then I turned it back on and tuned in KRCK FM. The DJ blabbered something about "Party Town Saturday Night!" I turned it off and looked for a CD. I wanted something quiet and gentle, something to calm me down. I found one of my mom's Dave Matthews CDs. I stuck it in, but before it even started I punched it back out.

———————————————

On the freeway, I seriously began to lose it. My brain, my thoughts—they spun wildly in every direction. For the first time in my life, I understood how extreme stress could drive your brain to impossible places. It could warp your thinking, pointing you in dangerous directions, which seemed to make perfect sense at the time.

That's how people kill themselves, I thought. *They get twisted around in their brain.*

I had to calm down. I tried the radio again and tuned in KKNR, the indie-rock station. A commercial was playing: *"I just saved a bunch of money on my car insur—."* I turned it off. I looked at my fists where they gripped the steering wheel. I thought I saw blood on my hands.

That was too much. That was the last straw. I simply could not be doing this: driving like a maniac, losing my mind, swerving through traffic with blood on my hands.

But I was. That was the thing. I *was*.

<hr />

I pulled into Jared's driveway. There was no one home, as I had hoped for and counted on. I turned off the car lights and killed the engine, praying the neighbors wouldn't wonder what the strange car was doing at the Fitches' house. I got out and hurried to the front door. It was unlocked. I went in and locked it.

The first thing to do was clean up. I clicked on the light and looked down at my shoes. There was blood on the toe of one of them. Or no, it was oil . . . or something. . . . It didn't matter. I yanked my shoes off. I took off my white socks, which had dark rings of dirt around the ankle. I stuffed the socks inside my shoes. I tiptoed barefoot into Jared's kitchen and found a plastic garbage bag under the sink. I put my shoes and socks in the bag.

Then, standing in the Fitches' kitchen, I peeled off my T-shirt and put it carefully in the plastic bag.

Then I noticed the window over the sink. It faced the street. The neighbors across the street could see me. I ducked down and slunk into the hall, where I couldn't be seen, and finished undressing. I didn't have a plan exactly, so I put all my clothes in the garbage bag.

I went into the closest bathroom. This was probably not the best idea, since it was Jared's mom's bathroom. But it was too late, I was already in it, it was already dirty, and I would have to clean it anyway.

I stood in the shower and turned on the water. When it hit me, black spots of grime splattered everywhere. I wiped down the shower curtain and the walls while I showered.

Once everything was clean, I closed my eyes and let the hot water beat on my back and neck. I tried to relax, or at least stop shaking. But it was hopeless. I couldn't stop. My lower lip trembled uncontrollably.

Then I started to cry. It happened suddenly, and

once it started I couldn't stop. The tears and sobs came pouring out of me. I cried and sobbed and moaned until I couldn't stand up anymore. I had to sit on the bottom of the tub while the hot water poured over the front of my head.

After I'd cried for a long time, I started to talk. I don't know who I was talking to. God maybe. I kept saying I was sorry. I didn't mean to do it. I asked why this had happened. What had I done to deserve this? I wasn't a violent person. I never got in fights. It wasn't fair. It was *so not fair.* . . .

After a few minutes, I thought I heard something in the house. I stood up. I shut off the water. I listened. But no, it was nothing. A heater had turned on. No one was there. It was just the unfamiliar house.

I stepped out and wrapped a towel around my waist. With a sponge from under the sink, I inspected every inch of the tub for black grime or blood or any clues of my being there. Then I picked up the garbage bag of my clothes and went downstairs.

In Jared's room I felt better. I felt the daring spirit of Jared around me. Crazy, insane Jared who did illegal stuff all the time. He was famous for it. For the first time, I had the thought: *Maybe I can get away with this.*

I quickly reminded myself that I would not be *getting away* with anything, since I hadn't really done anything. At least nothing that anyone in the same situation wouldn't have done. *It was an accident,* I reminded myself. It really was. It was nobody's fault. It was something that just happened.

I went to Jared's bureau and opened the top drawer. I needed clean clothes. I pawed through Jared's stuff. He was bigger than I was. He was a thirty waist. I found some boxer shorts. I held them up, looked at them.

Would I tell Jared?

No.

Possibly.

Maybe.

I would decide that later. I slipped on the boxers. They were loose but wearable. I went back to the bureau and found some baggy shorts and put them on. I found a big Rampage hoodie and some thick white socks and put those on. I clicked on Jared's boom box and tuned it to KEX. The weatherman said it would rain later. That was good, I thought, rain would cover things. It would cover footprints and blood tracks. Rain made things new again.

Then, in my mind, clear as a video replay, I saw the security guard getting pulled down under the train. I saw him get folded up like a rag doll. Then I saw the other picture: the body, mangled, severed, half of him on one side of the tracks, half on the other. I sat on

Jared's bed and burst into tears, swallowing and gasping and moaning all over again. I cried for several moments, then stopped. I had no tears. I was cried out. I had nothing left.

❧❧❧ ❧❧❧ ❧❧❧ ❧❧❧ ❧❧❧ ❧❧❧

I fell asleep on Jared's bed with my clothes on. I dreamed I was in a police station, sitting on a chair, in a hallway. But it wasn't exactly a police station; it was more like a hospital. Nurses even walked by. As I sat, I tried to decide if I should stay or go; there was still time to leave since I hadn't given my name yet. Then a woman was brought in. She was in handcuffs, and she had a terrified look on her face. They were taking her to the basement, where they operated on you, where they took things out of you, against your will. . . .

I woke up with a start. My forehead was damp with sweat. Outside, it was still dark. The rain fell gently on the trees outside Jared's window.

Jared. What about him? He broke the law all the time. He didn't think anything of it. Skaters' code. Skater law. Cops suck. Never tell a cop anything. Never help a cop in any way.

I lay back on the bed and blinked at the ceiling above me. I liked how warm I felt, how safe I felt in

Jared's room. I liked the sound of the rain. It reminded me of being younger, a little kid, sitting at the window, all the dreams you had when you were young, all the hopes for your future. . . .

I was so screwed.

I sat up and glanced around the room. *I was so screwed.* What was I going to do?

I shouldn't waste time. I needed to talk to someone. I needed to take action and get this weight off me. My dad. That was the person to talk to. I knew where he was—at my uncle Tommy's. I turned on the light and found Jared's portable phone. I could already feel the relief of telling him. . . .

I dialed my uncle's number. But I couldn't remember the last four numbers. I tried again. But I still couldn't remember. I dialed 411. The automated voice gave me my uncle's number. It offered to connect me for fifty cents but it was Jared's phone, so I hung up and dialed it myself. I waited. My heart began to pound. It connected. My heart thudded in my chest. It rang once . . . twice. . . .

I hung up.

But that was stupid. What was I doing? I had to call my dad. I started to dial it again, and again I stopped.

No. Don't involve your family. They didn't do it.

They're innocent. I should call the police myself.

But who was I kidding? There was no way I was calling the police myself. I started to cry again. The sound of the rain was what did it. The sad, lonely, far-away sound of the rain. I flicked off the light and went back to the bed and lay down with the phone cradled to my chest. *Oh God, please help me*, I whispered, rocking slowly on the bed. *Please, please, God help me.*

⊱⊰⊱⊰⊱⊰⊱⊰⊱⊰⊱⊰⊱⊰⊱⊰

I slept fitfully, dozing in and out. At seven A.M., I woke up completely and got ready to leave Jared's. But I didn't dare show up at my own house that early. It would be suspicious. I had to stay at Jared's. I tried watching TV, but it was Sunday morning, and it was all religious stuff and infomercials. I finally found some skate videos of Jared's and put those on. I didn't watch them, though. I couldn't focus on anything.

Finally, at eight thirty, I headed home. I stashed the garbage bag of my clothes in my mom's car and drove back to my own neighborhood. I knew of a Dumpster behind Mario's Pizza near my house. I stopped there, pulling into the back parking lot. It was Sunday morning, Mario's was closed, so no one was around. I casually took the bag of clothes out of my car and tossed it in. Then I drove to my parents' house.

My mom and brother were both up. I could hear the TV on in the living room. I prayed to God my mother wasn't in the kitchen. She wasn't. I walked through the kitchen and skipped up the stairs.

My mom heard me. She called out, asking what I was doing home so early.

"We didn't go to the Expo," I yelled back. "Jared got sick."

"What did he get sick with?"

"I'm not sure," I yelled, and kept going up. I hurried down the hall to my room and shut the door. I tore off Jared's clothes and quickly put on my own. I pulled on my other jeans and some old Adidas I had in my closet. I put on my own green OREGON sweatshirt.

It felt good to be home, in my own room, in my own clothes. It was a relief. Sort of.

"Honey!" called my mom. Her footsteps came down the hall toward my room. The door opened. "Honey?" she said, staring at me, studying my face.

"What?" I said, sitting quickly on my bed.

"Uncle Tommy called earlier. He said he got a call on his caller ID."

"He did?" I said.

"It said it was from the Fitches'. He asked me if I knew anyone of that name, and I told him that's where you were staying."

"Oh," I said.

"Did you call Uncle Tommy's?"

"Oh . . . uh . . ." I thought for a moment. "Yeah, maybe I did, by accident."

"He said the call was at four thirty in the morning."

"Huh," I said. "That's weird."

"Were you still awake then?"

"No," I said, trying to think. "But you know what? That's when Jared first woke up. Because he was sick. And so . . . I guess I was thinking about calling Ryan and seeing if he wanted to go . . . but then . . . I must have been half asleep or something. . . ." I tried to smile. "Maybe I was sleepwalking."

"What did you guys do last night?"

"Nothing. Just getting ready for the Expo. I wanted to see the new snowboards."

The phone rang down the hall. "Henry, would you get that, please?" my mom yelled to my little brother.

I sat watching my mother.

"Were you trying to call Dad?" she asked me seriously. "Be honest."

"No, I just . . . I must have dialed it by accident. . . ."

"Is there something you want to talk to him about? Something about the separation?"

"No," I said, "I just . . . it was an accident . . . calling Uncle Tommy, I mean."

"Because you can talk to him, you know. At any time. We all need to keep the lines of communication open."

"I know."

"I should call over there myself," said my mom, her face growing concerned. "I need to talk to Aunt Renee. . . ."

"Mom! It's for you!" yelled Henry from down the hall. My mother left the room.

I remained where I was, sitting on my bed, shaking.

⊱━━━━━━━━━━━━━━━━⊰

I tried to lie down. But I couldn't keep still. Henry had the TV blaring downstairs. I couldn't stand the sound of it, coming up through the floor. I started to freak out. I couldn't stay in my room.

I decided to go to the mall. I told my mom I wanted to go look at some snowboards, since I hadn't been able to at the Winter Expo.

That was okay with her, but she needed the car, so I had to walk. Which was fine.

"Where's your skateboard?" she asked as I headed out the door.

"I left it at Jared's," I said, going out of the house.

But that wasn't a very good excuse, I realized, as I walked down the driveway. People knew I always had my skateboard.

I walked toward Woodridge Mall. It was a long walk—too far, really; I should have gone the other way and taken the bus.

But I walked. The gray clouds hovered low in the sky. Raindrops began to fall. I wished I had a radio; I wanted to hear the news.

At the mall, I went straight to the magazine store. That day's papers were there. I bought *The Oregonian* for fifty cents and took it to Burger King. I sat and flipped through the pages. There was nothing in the main section about the security guard, nothing in the metro section.

Maybe they would think it was an accident. Maybe they'd think the guard was goofing around on the job. Or he was drunk. Or he just got too close to the train. People had accidents on the job. It was possible.

I suddenly thought about Scratch. I hadn't thought about him all night. Scratch. What kind of person has a name like *Scratch*?

At least he was smart. He was probably halfway to Phoenix by now. He was probably a thousand miles away. Guys like him knew what to do. You don't turn yourself in. You vanish. He'd beat up some cop in San Diego, and what had he done? Panicked? Called the po-lice? Went crying to his mother? No, he skipped town, he laid low. That's what they did in the *Godfather* movie. When the Al Pacino character killed that guy, they just sent him to Italy to chill. You don't panic. You just hunker down and keep your cool and don't do anything stupid.

"Hey," said someone. I looked up. It was Macy McLaughlin, a girl who lived on my street.

"Oh, hey," I said back. Macy was a sophomore, a year younger than me. She was with one of her sophomore friends.

"What are you doing here so early?" she asked.

"Nothing."

"What are you reading?"

"The newspaper."

She looked at me funny. She thought it was weird for me to be at the mall reading the newspaper in Burger King at ten in the morning. Which it was.

"I'm checking the sports scores," I said. "Then I have to get some stuff for my mom."

Macy studied me with her large brown eyes. She'd had a crush on me in sixth grade. She used to follow me around, leave notes in my locker. I didn't see her as much these days. She had become one of the cool sophomores. The girl with her was Rachel Simmons, another one of the cool sophomores.

"Okay," said Macy. "We gotta go."

"Okay," I said.

The two of them left. As they walked away, Macy looked back at me. It wasn't a giggly, crushy look; it was more checking on me. It weirded me out. I didn't want anyone looking at me like that. Not then.

Walking home from the mall, I thought about my parents. I couldn't tell the police, because my parents couldn't take it. They were already barely hanging on. Something like this, it would blow their world apart.

Especially my mom. She wasn't so stable. And my dad would go ballistic. They would blame each other. They would freak out and stop talking and then the divorce would start that much faster. The lawyers would use it against the other lawyers. My mother would have to think up an excuse for why I was running around loose on a Saturday night. It would kill her if she lost custody of us. She always said that she would never give up custody of Henry and me. Ever. She would do *anything*. She didn't care.

And my dad. It would look so bad. He leaves his wife, leaves his kids, and then this happens. The people at his work would think he was a terrible person. He might even get fired. It would make us all look horrible. It would be a total disaster, in every way.

For that reason, I decided I would do nothing. That was my new plan. I wouldn't even debate it. I would just do nothing for a day or two. Let the dust settle. Wait until my head cleared.

This new plan felt right. It calmed me down. That was a good sign all by itself. I said it over to myself: *Just chill for a day or two. Just let the dust settle.*

But the calm went away when I walked into our kitchen. On the refrigerator was a message: "Call Jared."

I went to my room. I didn't call Jared. I went online and tried a local TV news site. There were no reports about a dead security guard. I tried the Web site for the local paper. Nothing. I Googled various combinations of "murder," "body," "death," and "security guard" with "Portland, Oregon." Nothing came up. I deleted my search history and logged off.

Then I called Jared.

"Bro, what's up," he said. "Where you been?"

"Nowhere," I said. "At the mall."

"So, bro, guess what happened to me last night?"

"What?" I said.

"I totally got laid!"

"All right," I said, sitting on my bed. "Just like you planned it."

"But *not* just like I planned it," gushed Jared. "Because I almost got laid by her roommate, too!"

"You did?"

"Dude, there's so many hot college girls down there! You don't even know! And people were hooking up. I made out with *three* different girls. And nobody even cared. Nobody even noticed! I'm telling you man, college is the best!"

"Wow," I said.

"So check it out. So we're partying and everything, and we go back to Kelly's dorm and there's, like, a bunch of us . . . and her roommate starts dancing around, and doing this little striptease. And then she *flashes* us while the other girls weren't looking. I swear, it's like *Girls Gone Wild* down there. That's all they do is party and get naked!"

"Wow," I said again.

"Kelly, from the coffee shop, she was, like . . . I don't know . . . messed up or something. She's kind of a head case. But whatever. That's the thing: I coulda had my pick. Like this one blonde chick, she was totally checking me out, like from the minute I got there. . . ."

I tried to listen to his story. I tried to enjoy it. I needed to think about something else. I needed to get out of my own head.

". . . but I'm telling you," Jared was saying, "I am *so* going to college. You should have seen the frat we were at. Dudes had a flat-screen TV that, like, covered an entire wall. And kegs everywhere. And this pole you could slide down in the backyard—it was like a friggin' fire station!"

He kept talking. It sounded fun, but it sounded so far away. It sounded like a place I'd never get to.

"So what did you end up doing?" he finally asked. "Did you go to Paranoid?"

"No, I . . . I just ended up . . . hanging out."

"Did you call Jennifer?"

"Nah, I just hung out."

"Dude, seriously, if you had been down there with me, you coulda had *any* of those girls. Because they're, like, freshmen and nobody pays attention to 'em. I mean, the really hot ones get hit on. But the other ones. There are, like, so many doable chicks down there, just looking for someone to party with."

"Yeah," I said. "Sounds pretty easy."

"Bro, it's *totally* easy," said Jared. "So wait, did you sleep here last night?"

"Yeah."

"Huh. Cause there's this big black footprint on my mom's carpet. Right by the front door."

"Oh," I said. I stood up. "That must have been me. I think I stepped in something."

"My mom's not going to be psyched."

"Can you clean it up?"

"Dude, what am I? Your maid? You clean it up!"

"No. I will. I totally will. I mean . . ."

"Nah, I'm kidding. The cleaning lady will deal with it. But hey, do you have my Rampage sweatshirt? I can't find it."

"Yeah, I borrowed it."

"What'd you do that for?"

"My . . . mine got wet."

"So what exactly did you do last night? Just wander around by yourself?"

"Yeah, kinda, I mean . . . You know, I can't really talk right now. But I'll bring your sweatshirt to school tomorrow."

"Bro, I'm not really into you borrowing my clothes. Or going through my stuff. You didn't even *ask*."

"No, I know, I would have, I just—"

"You borrow anything else?"

"Uh . . . just some shoes."

"Some shoes? Which shoes?"

"Those old Etnies."

"Dude, what happened to you? You're borrowing my *shoes*? Did you borrow my underwear?"

"No," I lied, "I just . . . I just got a little wet. And I stepped in something. And I didn't want to track it all over your house."

"Just gimme my stuff back. Bring it to school tomorrow. And what's going on with Jennifer?"

"Nothing. I don't know exactly."

"Well if that's not happening, you should definitely check out Oregon State. I'm serious. I'm gonna need a wingman. I'm not even going to waste my time with stupid high-school girls anymore, not with that kinda action around."

"No, yeah, it sounds cool," I said, trying to sound like my old self. "It sounds awesome."

That night I went to bed at ten thirty, which was early for me. I turned off the lights and lay in my bed.

I didn't sleep. I lay staring at the floor in the dark. I was tired, more tired than I had ever been. But sleep was impossible. So I got up and pulled my chair to my window and sat, looking at the trees in our backyard.

I dug out an old Walkman and tuned it to KEX. Surely there would be something about the security guard. It had been twenty-four hours.

But there wasn't. The big news of the night was they had hired a new Portland Trail Blazers coach. The newspeople acted like it was the biggest event ever. I couldn't believe how much they went on about it. So they had a new coach. Big deal.

I kept tuning my Walkman to different stations. I listened to bits of music. I listened to bits of talk radio. I stared at the trees.

Then I got mad. It made me mad that people always talked about helping teenagers. There was always some new program, some new plan to help kids. There were ads on TV, on the radio. Hotlines, and this and that. But did any of it work? Not in the slightest. Here I was, with a real problem, with a serious problem, but was there anywhere *I* could go? Who do you call when something *really* goes wrong? Those geeks in the student-counseling office? When you had a real problem, there was nothing you could do, no one you could talk to. It was so typical. And so unfair. Why didn't they set up an anonymous number you could call, so you could talk to someone who actually knew something, someone who could give you real advice and tell you what your options were?

For once in my life I genuinely needed help, and where could I go? There was nowhere. There was nothing. And it really pissed me off.

Later, I fell asleep in my chair. I still had my Walkman headphones on, and I must have heard something about a murder. I woke up instantly and turned up the volume. But it wasn't local. It was the national ABC news. They were talking about a boy in Texas, a seventeen-year-old who had shot his next-door neighbor. He had been sentenced to death and was going on death row. His lawyers were appealing to the Texas Supreme Court; they wanted to get his sentence reduced to life in prison. They said it could take ten years of appeals.

I thought about that. Ten years. Death row. Life sentence. I pulled the headphones off my head and let them drop to the ground. What was I supposed to do?

What was I supposed to do?

Dear ____,

So that was the first day.

The next day I went to school. I was a total zombie. I stumbled onto the bus, stumbled to my locker. I was so in shock I barely knew where I was.

In math I didn't have my assignment. I hadn't done it, hadn't looked at it. Mr. Minter got kinda pissed. I had an A in math up till then.

At lunch I sat with my friends Parker and James. They talked about some Japanese horror movie they had seen. I didn't say anything. Then, as I ate, tears suddenly came into my eyes. The veggie burger I was eating turned to mush in my mouth. I felt so sad and so exhausted. Everything was like a terrible dream I kept waiting to wake up from. But I never did.

Parker and James took off, and I ended up eating by myself. I looked down the table and saw Macy McLaughlin. She was with some other sophomores. They looked so young to me, sitting there, gabbing about whatever. Macy turned in my direction and I quickly looked down into my food. But I thought about her: I remembered how she followed me around in sixth grade. She was really outgoing back then. She would follow me on her bike, pestering me, asking me endless questions. She wasn't like that now. She stayed with her cool friends. I thought about that for, like, twenty seconds—which I was grateful for. That was twenty seconds I wasn't seeing that security guard lying in the tracks.

After fifth period, I walked by Jennifer's locker. She had first lunch that day, so I hadn't seen her. She was on her cell phone, and she kept flipping her hair. When she finished talking, she didn't look to me. She bent down to get something out of the bottom of her locker. "So did you and Jared have fun on Saturday?" she asked.

I slipped my hands in my pockets. "Not really."

"What did you guys do?" she asked.

"Nothing. Just . . . hung out. . . ."

"You should have come with us. We went to Elizabeth's house and went swimming."

I nodded.

"But I guess that doesn't really interest you very much," she said. "I guess skating with Jared is more fun."

"I already told him I would."

That was the weird thing about Jennifer. She could be a little hard on you sometimes. But then she would turn around and be nice again.

"What are you doing after school?" she asked.

"Nothing."

"We could do something if you want."

"Okay," I said.

~~~~~~~~~~~~~~~

After school, I got my books and walked behind the cafeteria to meet Jennifer. Jared was skating with Christian Barlow and Paul Auster in the parking lot. They were the other two serious skaters at our school, besides Jared. They practiced kick-flips, ollies. I watched for a minute.

"Where's your board?" asked Jared, coming over.

"Left it at home."

"Why'd you do that?"

"I dunno," I said.

"What are you doing now?"

"Hanging out with Jennifer."

Behind him, Paul Auster landed a kick-flip. Christian tried one but couldn't land it. Jared pushed across the parking lot and tried one, too, but he fell on his ass.

Jennifer and I went to her house. No one was home, and we went upstairs to her bedroom. She seemed really excited about something, and when we got in her room she shut the door and jumped on her bed.

"So guess what happened to Petra?" she asked, bouncing on the bed. Petra was one of her friends.

"What?"

"She did it! With Mike Paley! They did it, like, three times last weekend."

"Wow," I said. Petra and Mike Paley had only been going out for a couple weeks.

"Do you think that's too soon?" she asked, still bouncing.

"I don't know," I said. I sat in her chair and looked at the stuff on her desk.

"I think it is," gushed Jennifer. "Kinda. But maybe not. Nobody really knows about it yet. She hasn't told that many people. But still. Can you believe that? Petra and Mike! And Maddy did it last summer. It's, like, totally happening to all my friends!"

Jennifer jumped up from her bed and went to her closet. She stood in front of a long mirror inside the door and brushed her hair. She had beautiful long blonde hair.

I watched her. I breathed a low sigh. I could still feel that ache in my chest. It was always there. No matter what else was happening.

"So now everyone's asking *me*," said Jennifer seriously.

"Yeah?"

"They want to know when I will. And if I want it to be with you."

I swallowed. "What do you tell them?"

"I say I don't know. I barely even know if you want to be my boyfriend." She held her hair and brushed it. "I mean, if you'd rather go skateboarding than hang out with me . . ."

"I told you—" I said, but I felt dizzy all of a sudden. My head swam. I felt choked in by the overstuffed room, the frilly comforter, the stuffed animals. It was too hot in there. It felt like the heat was on full blast.

Jennifer went back to the bed and sat down. "Don't you want to sit on the bed?" she asked, a huge grin on her face. "It's more comfortable."

I left the chair and sat on the bed. She was right, it was more comfortable. She grinned and scooted closer. She kissed me once on the lips. But when she felt my neck she stopped. "You feel hot," she said. "Are you okay?"

"I think so."

"You're not sick, are you?" said Jennifer. "I have cheerleader tryouts; I can't get sick."

"I'm okay," I said. But I felt weak. I wanted to lie down. I scooted farther onto her bed and lay on my back.

Jennifer looked thoughtfully at my body. "I mean for me, deciding who's your first, it's more about trust." She bounced on the bed. "And, like, if you know the person isn't going to run around talking about it, like it's this big conquest—"

The room spun a whole circle. I thought I was going to throw up. I sat up suddenly.

"Are you okay?" said Jennifer, alarmed.

"Sorry, I just feel dizzy."

She put her hand on my forehead. "You feel really hot. Maybe you have a fever."

"No, I just haven't slept. I'm just tired."

"Here, lie back," she said. A look of genuine concern came over her face. She lay back with me. She scooted close and began stroking my hair and my forehead. It felt nice. I closed my eyes.

We lay like that for a long time. Whatever was happening stopped, and I felt better. Then she kissed my cheek, and my temple, and the side of my head. Then she got up and turned the light down.

She lay next to me. She ran her hands across my

chest and unbuttoned the front of my shirt. She crawled on top of me and we started making out. It got pretty intense, but then I started to freak out again. I felt vulnerable and exposed, like someone might be looking for me, someone might be tracking me down.

I sat up suddenly.

"What?" she said. "Now what's wrong?"

"Nothing, I just . . . I gotta go."

She was losing her patience. "Do you not want to be my first?" she asked.

"No . . . I just . . . I don't know. . . ."

She got up. She crawled off the bed and ran into her bathroom and slammed the door. I heard the water turn on.

I sat on the bed for a moment. But I didn't want to stay in that house any longer. I couldn't take this. Not now.

I found my Vans, which I had kicked off. I put my shirt back on and straightened my pants. I looked at myself in her mirror. I looked terrible. I looked totally guilty.

I went to the bathroom door. "Jennifer?" I said, tapping the door slightly with my knuckle.

"*What?!*" she said. She sounded very upset.

"I think I might be sick. Or have a fever or something. We can talk about this later. I'm just not myself today."

"I wish I could believe you."

"You gotta believe me. I swear."

"Why can't you at least talk to me? God, you're the worst boyfriend ever!"

I was in no condition to argue. "I'm sorry," I said. "I'm gonna go. I'll see you tomorrow."

I left her room and found my way out the front door. Usually I skated home from her house. But I had no skateboard, so that day I walked.

Back at my house, I began thinking about confession. I had never been, but I had seen it on TV. And my dad was Catholic. He never went to church or anything, but I thought maybe since he was, that would make me qualified to go.

The main thing was, at confession, you could tell the priest the worst thing you ever did, and they couldn't tell anyone. They didn't see your face, so they didn't even know your identity. You were completely safe. And then afterward, the priest told you some things to do, like help the poor or whatever, and then you were forgiven and you felt better.

And also, then God would know you were really sorry, which would be good. There was just one problem: I didn't know if I believed in God. Like when I cried in Jared's mom's shower, I felt like I was talking to God. But when I actually thought about it, I didn't know what I believed. My parents didn't do religious stuff. Like, my dad said he believed in God, but then he would joke and say you might as well because if he didn't exist you were screwed anyway.

So I didn't know. But I thought confession would be good. I needed to tell someone. And it was at least one thing I could do while I tried to figure out my options. And maybe you could talk to the priest about it. Maybe you could ask him for advice.

That night, I ate dinner with my little brother Henry. I watched him read a graphic novel from the library, but he kept spilling milk on it. That was the thing. People did bad things all the time. They wrecked library books. They cheated in school. They beat up the nerdy kids.

I tried to eat. I had hardly eaten anything since Saturday. I still thought constantly about calling the police. I had this daydream of walking into a police station and turning myself in. How dramatic it would be. Everyone would say how brave and honest I was. And of course they would be totally nice to me, like in the movies. The kindly old sergeant would get me a Coke and sit me down with the lady counselor who would say, "It's completely normal that you were afraid to tell us. That's what usually happens in cases like this—the person comes in days later. Don't worry, you did the right thing—it was an accident. That security guard endangered your life. We have lots of reports of him harassing innocent skateboarders like yourself. . . ."

At the same time, I had another dream, a nightmare really, of being bullied and pushed around, of hard adult faces turning on you like they do. Male faces, turning ugly and grabbing you and handcuffing you and not telling the truth about things. And then some politician using you: telling everyone how evil teenagers were, skateboarders especially, and they had to be stopped! We're going to make you an example! That stuff happened, too. I had seen it. Every skateboarder had.

After dinner in my room, I Googled "confession." The first thing that came up was an article about a priest in Minnesota who turned a child molester in to the police, after he confessed. It was a big controversy and all these other people had written comments about whether the priest should have told or not. Most people said he should have. Most people agreed that child molesting was worse than breaking the pact of

the confessional. But other people thought that anything a person confessed, even murder, was protected
no matter what. You weren't even talking to the priest,
they believed—you were talking to God. The priest was
just a stand-in.

There were more articles about controversial
priests. In Massachusetts, a whole town was suing one
priest, and it got so bad the parish declared bankruptcy
and sold the church. Then I found this conspiracy Web
site that said the pope was trying to make everyone go
into credit-card debt so he could take over the World
Bank. Everything I clicked on just got worse and worse.
Maybe confession wasn't such a good idea

I gave up after a few minutes and lay down on my
bed. Then my mom knocked on my door and came into
my room. She was all flustered because my dad had
come over. He was in the garage packing stuff up. She
said he wanted to talk to me.

<hr />

I didn't trust myself to talk to my dad. I didn't know
what I would say. So before I left my room, I made a
decision: Since I didn't know if I should tell him, I
wouldn't. And then later, if I decided I should tell him,
I still could.

The important thing was, I couldn't break down

and start bawling and blurt it out. That would be the worst situation, because then the firestorm between him and my mom would begin. And that would be too brutal to think about.

I went downstairs. I grabbed a couple carrot sticks off Henry's plate as I went through the kitchen.

The garage was cold that night. I sat on the step and watched my father dig through the big storage closet. When he stood up, he held a small, single-burner Coleman stove. My heart sank when I saw that. We had used it when Henry and I and my dad went fishing two summers ago. It was the last thing we did together before everything fell apart.

Looking at that Coleman stove, I had a strange thought: *I might need that.* But for what? When I ran away? When I tried to camp my way to Canada?

"Hello there," said my dad, when he noticed me watching him.

"Hey," I said back.

He saw me looking at the Coleman stove. "I wondered where this was," he said.

"Are you going to take that?"

"I'm just going to borrow it. Uncle Tommy and I are going to the lake this weekend."

I sat and watched my dad in the fluorescent garage light.

He set the camp stove down. He brushed the dust from his hands. "I wanted to talk to you," he said. "I'm not sure what you've heard, exactly. Or what your mother is telling you. I may not be coming back here anymore."

I killed someone, Dad. The words bounced through my head. I didn't say them, of course.

"We're still, you know, discussing things," he continued, "and trying to work out logistics. And do what's best for you and Henry. It's not easy trying to work with your mother. As I'm sure you know . . ."

I nailed him with my board, Dad. I cracked him in the head.

". . . So I wanted to check in with you, see how you were doing," he said calmly. "I mean, obviously it's hard. It's certainly not an ideal situation." My dad studied the shelf in the storage closet as he said this. He was looking for other things he might need at the lake. "So, is there anything you want to say? Any considerations you have?"

I watched him. He began to move paint cans to the side. He found a flashlight.

"I don't know," I said. "Not really."

"Well . . . I guess that makes sense. The whole situation . . . is so difficult." He stared into the front of the flashlight and tried the switch. It lit up. "How's school, by the way? How are your classes?"

"Okay."

"How are Parker and those guys?"

"They're fine."

"I saw Parker's dad the other day at Outdoor World."

"Yeah?" I said.

"You still skateboarding?"

"Sometimes."

He set the flashlight next to the camp stove. Then he turned back into the closet.

I killed someone, Dad. He attacked me, but I kept my head and waited for my moment and I took him out. Could you do that, Dad? If you had to?

He dug through some gardening stuff. I cleared my throat and stood up. "I actually have some homework," I said.

He looked at me. He shrugged helplessly. "I'm really sorry about this, son. I really am. I never wanted something like this to happen."

"I know the feeling," I said back.

"All I really want to say is . . . Well . . . if there's anything I can do . . . any way I can help you . . ."

"Can you bring the stove back?" I asked.

He gave me a surprised look. "What are you going to do with it?"

"I dunno. Go camping."

"Yeah, sure, I'll bring it back," he said.

But I didn't think he would.

⊷⊶⊷⊶⊷⊶⊷⊶⊷⊶⊷⊶⊷⊶⊷⊶⊷

The next day at school, I slipped into the library before class and grabbed the newspaper. I took it to one of the back tables so the librarian wouldn't see me. I flipped through it slowly, scanning each page. I looked for anything—accidents, deaths. A Hispanic man had been hit by a car in Hillsboro. A house burned down in Northeast. A mayor of a small town on the coast had taken some bribes for something. And of course there was tons of stuff about the new Trail Blazers coach.

But nothing else. I folded up the paper and put it back without letting the librarian see me. Then I went to class.

Before lunch that day, a bunch of people played football in the back parking lot. I got on Parker's team, and he threw me three touchdown passes. We kicked ass. It was the first time I actually smiled in days.

Then at lunch, I felt hungry again, for the first time since Saturday night. I ate all my food, had seconds, then ate all of Parker's and James's food. I told them I'd had a stomach virus and hadn't been able to eat. They said I looked a little weird on Monday.

Later, Jennifer came by my locker, and I was actually happy to see her. She was being flirty and cute and just for the hell of it I gave her a big kiss, right there in the hall—which got her all giggling and hopping around like she does.

I felt like everything was right with the world again. Or I did until I took my world literature test. I had totally forgotten about it. I mean, I wasn't so great in English anyway. It was this book called *Notes from the Underground*, and I hadn't even bought the book. So I got burned on that. But I told Mrs. Hall I was sick all weekend, and she said I could take it again next week if I wanted. I figured I could get the SparkNotes and do a makeup.

Then after school, Jared and some of those guys were playing S-K-A-T-E on the steps by the parking lot. I sat on the steps and watched.

"Bro, where's your board?" Jared said, when he saw me.

"Home."

"You don't bring it to school anymore?"

"I don't have room in my locker," I said.

"What are you talking about?" he said, sneering like this was the stupidest thing he had ever heard.

"I dunno, I just . . . didn't feel like bringing it."

Right then, Christian Barlow ollied the lower steps. Everyone stopped to watch him ride it into the parking lot.

Jared immediately spun his board and took off, to see if he could match it. He couldn't; he bailed and got a "K."

I watched the other guys try to ollie the lower steps. Paul Auster fell on his ass and smashed his hand. He was in serious pain, rolling around, holding his wrist between his legs.

Jared tried it again, for the hell of it, and bailed again and ran into the parking lot.

"This is lame," he said, retrieving his board. "We should go to Paranoid."

"Paranoid Park?" said Christian Barlow.

"Sure," said Jared.

"That place is skanky," said Christian.

"Bro! Paranoid kicks ass!"

"Yeah, if you, like, just got out of jail," said someone else. "Some guy got stabbed there."

"It's rad, though," said Jared. He looked at me to confirm this.

I shrugged. "I only went there once."

"Yeah, but you liked it," said Jared. "We should all go. This weekend. We could go there right now."

Christian didn't want to. Paul had no opinion. I couldn't. "I gotta hang out with Jennifer," I said.

"Yeah?" said Jared. "You got anything off her yet?"

"Not really," I said.

He laughed. "What? Is she giving you the good-girl treatment?"

"Nah, she's just . . . you know."

"I'd do her," said Paul Auster. "With that body? And you know she wants it."

"All those girls," said Christian. "Petra practically attacked Mike Paley."

"It hasn't really developed that far," I said, trying to defend myself.

But nobody cared anyway; they were all waiting for Christian to do his next trick.

━━━━━━━━━━━━━━━

The next couple days were more of the same. At school, I'd have an hour or two when I would feel like myself. I'd play hoops or hang out or whatever. Then at some unexpected moment—at my locker, or sitting in class— I'd remember the security guard. I'd see him in front of me, mangled on the tracks. Sometimes I could get away and go sit in a stall in the bathroom for a few minutes. But other times I'd be stuck with it.

Home was the same. I'd kill time, try to stay occupied. I would play video games for a couple hours, watch some TV, even do a little homework. Then it was up to bed. That was the hardest part. At least I was sleeping better now. I started taking these allergy pills my mom got me. If you took a couple, they kinda knocked you out.

Then on Thursday morning, on my way to school, I noticed this church down the road from my school. It was in this big building that used to sell lawn mowers and gardening stuff. I figured it probably wasn't a very good church if they put it in an old lawn mower shop. But it made me think about the church thing again.

So that day after school, I took the bus downtown to the church my family went to on Christmas. It was weird being downtown. I hadn't been there since Saturday. Getting off the bus, I was checking all around like I was a fugitive. When I saw a cop car, my whole body froze up.

But I kept moving and eventually found the church. It was a big stone building with thick oak doors. The lawn out front was perfectly groomed, with flowers and green grass and little walkways on the sides.

I went up the smooth stone steps in front. I pulled open the heavy door and instantly got an eerie feeling in my stomach. Inside, it was quiet, hushed; the red carpet was spongy under my feet. I proceeded cautiously forward.

No one seemed to be there. Which seemed odd. It was totally empty. Was that possible? Wasn't there supposed to be someone there?

I figured you must be allowed in, since the door was open. I crept forward and looked around. It was completely empty.

I didn't want to go too far inside. I sat on one of the benches, near the back. They were beautiful polished wood. Everything was super nice. I started to wonder if a priest in a high-class church like this would understand something like what happened to me. Probably stories involving skateboarders and Paranoid Park and people named "Scratch" were not their specialty.

I sat. I stared forward. The quiet and the stillness started to get to me. For some reason I thought of Henry. I pictured him at home, ignored, overlooked, crashed in front of the TV night after night. No Dad. Mom freaking out. His big brother locked in his room with his own terrible secrets. My family: We were disintegrating.

I started to cry. There was already so much pain in

the world. And what had I done? I had made it worse. I had made it so much worse.

After I'd cried, though, I felt better. And then I started having strange thoughts. I looked around and wondered why people didn't steal stuff from churches. There was no one supervising, and there was all this stuff—benches and books, maybe some of the metal stuff was gold. I checked the ceiling for cameras. I was glad I hadn't said anything out loud. They probably thought I was some kid crying because my dog died. I wish my dog *had* died. But no, I didn't wish that.

Then something even more weird happened. When I walked out of the church, I felt awesome. I felt like the biggest shitkicker. I strutted down the street like, *Don't mess with me, muthafucka.* I stared at these girls in the park like, *You think your boyfriends are tough? You don't know tough!*

But that was so evil and wrong, and just as suddenly, I felt so awful I could barely walk. *What was wrong with me?* I would have cried more, but I was cried out. I wondered how long it would take for this to wear off. I tried to imagine myself in five years, or ten; would I ever be able to just walk down the street?

And that was the *best*-case scenario. There was still the possibility of getting caught.

I walked more. I watched the downtown people heading home from work. They wore suits and business clothes and got into nice cars. They probably had stuff in their past—mistakes, bad things they'd done. Everyone must. I thought about soldiers in Iraq, in Vietnam, and every other war. They *had* to kill people. And they had to live with it. Soldiers through all of history did. And it wasn't like killing people was some bizarre event that never happened. Someone got killed on TV every two point five minutes. All you did in video games was kill people.

But what were you supposed to do with that weight? Once it was on you? Just be a man? Just suck it up? Maybe you were. Maybe that was the real test. Maybe that's exactly the thing that *made* you a man: the ability to function with the worst possible secrets in your brain. Which was why so many grown-up men seemed so ridiculous. They'd never felt that weight. They never felt that responsibility. They were untested, unproven; they were boys in grown-up clothes.

They were like my dad.

<hr/>

There was a big party at Christian Barlow's on Friday. Jennifer bugged me about it all week.

I went early to hang out with Jared and check out the half-pipe Christian had built in his backyard. I didn't have a board so I bummed Jared's, but I totally sucked. I couldn't do anything. After I fell on my ass a couple times, I gave up and sat in the grass with the non-skaters. That was okay, though; it was a perfect late-September evening—warm, with the smell of leaves in the air. People could tell it was the last of the summer. Everyone was kicking back. I tried my best to enjoy it.

Then Macy McLaughlin showed up. She was with her cool sophomore friends. They stayed in their little pack, not talking to anyone. They were all dressed up, trying to look good for the upperclassmen.

When Macy saw me, she came over. "Hey," she said.

"Hey," I said back.

She looked at the half-pipe. "How come you're not skating?"

"Don't feel like it."

Another of her friends walked over. They both stood there. I was lying in the grass, my head on Jared's board.

"You guys can sit down if you want," I said.

They didn't want to. They had to go inside with their friends.

I watched them walk away. It was weird how the

younger kids come up. I remembered my first parties, standing around, trying to look cool, trying to act like I knew what I was doing.

Those were the kinds of problems you're supposed to have when you're young.

⊱⊱⊱⊱⊱⊱⊱⊱⊱⊱⊱⊱⊰

When it got dark, everyone moved inside. It was a good party. People seemed really happy and excited for the new school year. I looked around for Jennifer, but she hadn't shown up. So I wandered around and played foosball with some guys in the basement.

Jennifer arrived at about ten thirty. She and Petra made a big entrance. They had been at Elizabeth Gould's having "cocktails," and now they were drunk and wanted to dance and whoop it up. I avoided them. Instead I sat in the backyard with Jared and some other seniors. That's where Macy appeared again. She had momentarily lost her friends and came and sat next to me. We didn't really say anything, and then she saw her friends again and ran off.

When she was gone, Jared asked me who she was, and I said it was Macy McLaughlin, who lived down the street from me.

He said she was cute. The other guys agreed. They

were like, *Dude where did* she *come from?*

I was like, *Calm down, she's practically my kid sister.*

But they didn't care. They thought she was hot.

❧❧❧❧❧❧❧❧❧❧❧❧❧❧❧❧

Around midnight, Jennifer found me. She grabbed me by the hand and pulled me upstairs. She had apparently staked out a room to make out or whatever. It was someone's bedroom, a little girl's.

Jennifer locked the door and put her arms around me and made this big show of being the sexy girl who'd waited all night to get with her guy. She kept making sexy faces, like she was wild with passion.

It all happened pretty fast. We got on the bed and she crawled on top of me. At first, I was into it. She smelled good and it was easy to lose myself in the moment. But then I realized how serious she was. This was it. This was the big moment. She wanted to lose "it" tonight. She'd made up her mind.

I didn't try to stop her. I should have. The whole situation was so weird anyway. For most of it, I felt like I wasn't even there, like I was outside my body, floating above the whole thing. At one point I was like, *Please, God, just let this be over. I give up. I don't know how to be human. Everything I do is wrong, and everything else I do just makes it worse.*

Afterward, we snuggled, but even that seemed like an act. Everything people did was an act. People did what they thought they were supposed to do. Learn to kiss at fourteen. Learn to drive at fifteen. Learn to have sex at sixteen. Life was easy. Just follow the schedule, don't make any big mistakes, and everything will be fine.

Jennifer caressed the side of my head. "That was *amazing*," she breathed into my ear.

I nodded.

"Do you think we should do it again?" she asked, lifting her head. "Or do you want to wait? Maybe we should wait. We're going to need more condoms. We should go buy some. They have them at Rite Aid. That's where Petra and Mike get theirs."

She lay back down and turned onto her back. "You were so good," she sighed. "Was I good?"

"Yes," I answered. We lay like that for another few minutes. Then she got restless. "Oh my God, I have to go to the bathroom," she said. She went into the little bathroom beside the bed, stopping to dig her cell phone out of her jeans.

I could hear her in the bathroom. She dropped the

toilet seat down. I heard her dialing her cell phone. She squealed into it. "Yes! *Yes!*" she whispered. "We *totally* did it. . . . Oh my God, it was *fantastic!*"

I couldn't hear what else she said. I got up. I found my boxers and put them on. Jennifer flushed the toilet and came out. She picked up her clothes, too. "Should we go back downstairs?" she asked me.

"Sure," I said.

We went back to the party. As soon as we reached the bottom of the stairs, she ran into the living room to find her friends. I turned the other direction, to the backyard. There were still some people standing around the half-pipe in the dark. A freshman was on it, rolling back and forth, trying not to fall. I watched him. It soothed me somehow. Back and forth. Back and forth. Try not to fall. . . .

That whole weekend turned into an extended party. After Friday night, everyone went home and slept, and then the next day, Christian and Jared and a bunch of us went to Paul Auster's during the day to watch skate videos and play video games. Then we met Jennifer and Elizabeth and those guys for a matinee movie.

Jennifer was so happy. She was grinning super big, and all her friends stared at me and giggled. Elizabeth even said right in front of everyone, "So I guess you guys sealed the deal."

That night the whole gang of us drove around downtown. On Broadway there were the usual carloads of high-school kids yelling back and forth. We ran around and switched cars. I got in Elizabeth Gould's car with Jennifer and everyone teased us and made sex jokes. It was like Jennifer's official de-virginization party. She was the happiest I had ever seen her.

On Sunday, all the guys went to Skate City. I didn't want to show up without a board, so I got up early and drove my mom's car to the mall and got another board. I wanted to get the same deck and see if I could scuff it up or whatever—not that that would fool anyone—just to make it less obvious. But they didn't have it. I got one that was close and paid with my debit card. I had just enough money for it, thanks to the new allowance my dad gave me out of guilt.

So then I met everyone at Skate City. It was funny—with no girls around, nobody talked about Jennifer and me. Nobody cared. That's part of the skater thing. It's a place where you forget all that.

Then on Monday, I went to school and it was all about Jennifer again. She came to my locker and wanted to know if I'd gotten the condoms yet. I hadn't. Did I want to go get them after school? I wasn't sure. Maybe.

"What's the matter?" she said. "Are you mad?"

"No," I said.

She stared at me. "You sure act weird sometimes. And after what we did. You'd think you'd be a little more happy to see me."

"Hey, it was your idea," I said.

"*What?*" she said. She took a step back. "What does *that* mean?"

"Nothing."

"So having sex was *my* idea?" she whispered, angrily. "You didn't *want* to? You just *went along*?"

"No. No, I'm just saying, you were the one who wanted to get *the condoms*. So I thought we would get them together."

Jennifer accepted this. "Oh," she said. "Okay. I thought you were talking about something else."

"No, that's all I meant."

"Okay," she said. "Well . . . we'll do that."

"Okay then," I said.

Jennifer left me alone for the rest of the day. Then, before last period she told me she couldn't go; she had an appointment at the dermatologist. That was a relief.

With nothing to do, I found Jared and those guys and skated with them on the steps behind the cafeteria. That made me feel better. I felt like I was getting my skate-legs back. I liked my new board. I could do stuff again.

Later, while we sat around drinking Cokes, Jared told more details about his college trip and the weird college girl he hooked up with. He had told this stuff before, but people liked hearing it again. It was quite a story.

As I listened, I wondered if I would ever tell any-one about my night at Paranoid Park. It occurred to me that I never would. That was the only way. It would be in lockdown. Like when a submarine springs a leak and you have to seal off that part. I would lock down that part of my life. I would close it off and seal it. What else could I do? Risk trying to tell someone? Gamble my whole life on if the police and the lawyers and the judges decided a skater has a right to defend himself? I was sorry. I felt bad for the security guard and his family. But there was no fixing it now. It was done and over with. We all had to move on with our lives.

And if it weighed on me, if it meant some sleepless nights, well, that was a sacrifice I would make for the other people involved. For my parents, for my brother, for the people who had taught me and helped me and invested in my future.

For them, I would bear the burden. For them I would be a man.

Dear _____,

Having some coffee this morning. That's one thing I've learned here at Uncle Tommy's: how to drink coffee in the morning.

⊷⊷⊷⊷⊷⊷⊷⊷⊷⊷⊷⊷⊷⊷

But anyway—that was the situation. The first couple days were pure hell. The next couple totally sucked. Things got a little better after a week. And at ten days, well, the worst of it seemed to be over, the crisis had passed. I might walk around like a haunted zombie for the rest of my life, but at least I would *have* a life.

Then one night, I came out of the shower and stopped in the TV room to watch the end of *Crossing Jordan* with my little brother. I was drying my hair with a towel when a newsbreak came on. The newcaster lady said something about a scandal with the new Trail Blazers coach. Then she said, "And police now think that the body of a protection officer found dead at the train yard in southeast Portland last week may have been the victim of murder. Stay tuned for all these stories, sports, and weather at eleven." While she spoke, a little graphic of train tracks appeared beside her head.

Then there was a commercial for the new Honda Odyssey.

I sat stunned, unmoving. Henry sat on the other end, kicking at the base of the couch.

I tried to breathe. I couldn't. I tried to lift my arm, to continue to dry my hair, but I couldn't do that, either. I managed one short, stunted breath. On the TV, the Honda Odyssey had a family in it, a happy family, with a dog and kids watching TV screens in the backseat. My stomach tightened up so much I thought I was going to throw up.

I managed to stand up and walk to my room. I sat on my bed and gradually got my breath back. Then I went to my computer. If it was on TV, it would be online. I clicked on the local TV news Web site. It was the main story on their home page:

Train-yard Death Now Possible Homicide

Police department officials have reopened the case of Cole R. Stringer, the protection officer who was found dead in southeast Portland on the morning of September 18. Initially, police treated the death as an accident, but autopsy reports have now given the police cause to reexamine the case as a possible homicide.

Cole Stringer, a uniformed officer, was found dead inside the central train yard in the industrial district of southeast Portland. An employee of the Port of Portland, Stringer, 32, patrolled the train yard and its surroundings. Initial reports indicated that Stringer had become entangled in a moving freight train and was accidentally killed.

The Port of Portland is required by law to perform autopsies on deceased employees lost on the job. After evaluating the final report, Portland Police reopened the case.

"There is data in the autopsy that would indicate that there may have been other people involved," said Clyde Miller, director of communications for the Portland Police.

Anyone with information regarding the incident are instructed to call the Portland Police's hotline at 555-778-7778.

I read it once. I read it again. Then I clicked on "history" of my Web browser and saw that I had many local news and local crime Web sites up on my computer. I was getting sloppy. I clicked "delete history" and then checked back to make sure everything was gone.

I thought about other things. My dirty shoes and socks, where were they? In the Dumpster, probably safely gone by now. What about my mom's car? I had cleaned it the other night, scrubbing the seats and the pedals. How about my story? Who knew I went there that night? Jared. What had I told him? I told him I didn't go to Paranoid Park.

That was my story: I didn't go to the park. I had to remember that. I dropped him off, drove around, went back to his house. That was it. I did not go to Paranoid.

But what about my skateboard? Where was my skateboard? Could I say someone stole it? *Yes!* Someone stole my skateboard and used it in the crime! But no, if the police got that close, if they talked to other people at Paranoid that night, they would know it was me. How about Scratch? Could I blame it on him? He took my skateboard and *he* hit the guy! No, no, no, I couldn't blame it on someone else. What was I thinking? That was totally evil.

But maybe I could. Scratch was a street person. They wouldn't believe him. He wasn't going to college, he didn't live in a nice neighborhood, they would . . .

no, no, no . . . It was insanity. . . . I couldn't do more bad things. I had to do the right thing. I had to do the right thing, now, before I lost my nerve.

I went to my phone and picked it up. I dialed the police number. 555-788-7778, but that wasn't the right number. I turned back to my computer, but I had already deleted the site. I tried again. It was . . . 555 . . . 778-7788? That wasn't right, either. I tried again. 555-788-7888, but before it rang I hung up. But that was stupid, what if they had caller ID? What if they called me back?

I flew into a panic. I stood up and began pacing my room. Had I saved anything from that night? No. I still had Jared's jeans. I had to give those back. What about the people on the bridge? The two women? They hadn't noticed me. They were busy talking. What about the guy on the bike? He might have. We practically collided. And I was so dirty! How could they *not* notice me? But being dirty doesn't mean anything. I could be a mechanic or a guy working construction or something.

I paced. Again, in the midst of the terrible swirl of my brain, the concept came back to me: *Do the right thing.* I went back to the phone. I picked it up. I stared at the number pad. *I'm a kid*, I thought. *I'm sixteen. Kids screw up. Kids get scared. Nobody's going to care that*

*I didn't tell right away. I'll say I didn't know what hap-
pened. There was a scuffle and then we ran. We didn't
see him get killed. We didn't even know he got killed.*

Of course. That was perfect. "No, Officer," I'd say.
"We just pushed him and ran away. We didn't know he
got killed by the train. Only when I saw it on the news,
and then I knew I should call you right away."

Okay, that was good. Better to just get everything
out in the open. It was just manslaughter, right? Or
whatever you call it when someone accidentally gets
killed. And I'm a minor. And I didn't know! That was
the key. I didn't even know that he died!

I dialed the police. Then I slammed the phone down
again. No. What if something went wrong? What if
Scratch thought I snitched on him? He would kill me.
He would have friends in jail who would kill me. If I
told the cops about Scratch, I was taking a huge risk. I
had to leave Scratch out of it. If I could.

What about footprints? There must have been footprints at the scene of the crime. And blood. Did I track
blood somewhere? What about that sports car that saw
me skating away from the train tracks? I had totally
forgotten about that.

This was getting crazy. I had to calm down. I had to
refocus and think logically. Scratch was probably long

gone. He had a ten-day head start. He was probably a million miles away in Canada, or Mexico. And he was smart. Wherever he was, they would never find him.

What about witnesses? Who else was at Paranoid that night? The two friends of Scratch's. They would remember me. Paisley was the girl's name. And the other guy. I didn't remember his name. Maybe I never knew it.

More importantly: Did I tell them my name? No, I did not. Did I tell them I had a car? No, I lied and said I didn't. Did I tell them where I lived? No, I did not. *I didn't tell them anything because I was afraid of them and I didn't want them to know who I really was.* Okay, but would they remember what I looked like? Probably not—I was a Prep, completely ordinary; I looked like a million other high-school students.

But what if Scratch went back there? What if they were all together somewhere? And what if *they* get scared and decide to blame it all on me, to protect themselves?

It was a terrible night. I lay in bed, my brain spiraling downward, faster and faster, every possibility I could think of, every course of action, it would all end in disaster. I could feel the weight of it destroying me. No matter what I did, I had killed someone. There was no escaping that. Someone would tell, someone would remember me, something would go wrong. And then the police would come.

I thought about the police. It was really my fear of them that had stopped me from doing anything. But why didn't I trust the police? And why was I so quick to think of myself as a criminal? Why was I so sure this would all somehow go against me?

I had a revelation then, lying in bed in the dark: *I was a bad person.*

I was. I realized it all at once. That explained everything. *Character is fate.* My English teacher had written it on the board at the beginning of school. I had a bad character, I was a bad person, and now my fate had caught up to me.

In my mind I went through every bad thing I had ever done. I'd lied to people, I'd stolen stuff, I beat up Howie Zimmerman in fourth grade. I threw a shopping cart in the Clackamas River my freshman year. I kicked the side mirror off a car once when I'd crashed skateboarding. The list was endless. It covered every stage of my life. *I had just that weekend had sex with a girl I didn't even like!*

At dawn I fell asleep for a few minutes, and then the alarm went off. I had to go to school. I went to the bathroom and not even the hottest water in the shower could loosen the tightness in my back and neck. My whole body was like a throbbing knot. In the mirror, my face was swollen and blotched red. I looked so terrible I thought for sure my mother would say something.

But she had her own problems. I ate breakfast and avoided the newspaper that Henry had spread over the table. *I was a bad person.* I had accepted that over the night. I was evil and I would die and then I would be off the planet and that would be good. It would be good for me. It would be good for the planet.

Then I started to cry. I had to stand up and walk out of the room without letting anyone see my face. I ran down into the basement and fell onto the old couch, sobbing as quietly as I could.

"Honey?" my mother called down the stairs. "What are you doing? You're going to be late."

I had become very good at covering up. I instantly stopped crying, and in a perfectly reasonable voice, said, "Nothing, Mom, just looking for a book. Can I take your car to school?"

"You're going to have to if you don't hurry up. . . ."

"I know. I'm coming," I said. I dried my eyes with the back of my hand. I wiped the snot on one of the cushions. I took a deep breath and walked up the stairs.

My mom stopped me in the hall. "Honey, your eyes

are all red—are you all right?" The funny thing was, she thought it was her fault. She thought I was upset about the separation.

"I'm fine," I answered. "It's just allergies."

"Did you take those pills?"

"I did, but they make me so sleepy. I gotta go. Can I take your car?"

She gave me the keys and I hurried out. I threw my books in the front seat and sat in the car for a moment, trying to pull myself together.

That's when I saw Macy McLaughlin standing in the grass beside me.

Macy needed a ride to school. She had missed her bus. Could I take her with me?

That was about the last thing I wanted to do. But what could I say? I motioned for her to get in. She did, putting on her seat belt while I started the car. I backed down the driveway, but I went too fast and just missed taking out our mailbox. I had to take it easy.

I put the car into drive and started forward. But then Rufus, the neighbor's dog, dashed into the street right in front of me. I slammed on the brakes. "Get outta the street, you dumb dog!" I shouted.

Macy stared at me.

"Why can't people keep their stupid dogs in their stupid houses, where they belong?" I muttered.

Macy remained silent.

"What?" I said. "You saw him. He ran right in front of me!"

"I didn't say anything."

"And now he'll go knock over our garbage cans. And I'll have to clean it up."

"You're sure in a good mood this morning," she said. "What's wrong with your eyes?"

"Nothing. Allergies."

"I thought people got allergies in the spring," she said.

I didn't answer. I stopped at a red light. I turned on the radio. But I hated the radio now; I couldn't listen to anything for more than a few seconds. I turned it off.

"Actually, I'm supposed to ask you something," said Macy.

"Yeah? What?"

"My friend Rachel wants to buy her boyfriend a skateboard. For their anniversary."

I shook my head.

"What's wrong with that?" she asked.

"Skateboards aren't something a girlfriend can buy you."

"That's why she wanted to ask you."

"Nobody can buy you a skateboard," I said. "It's a personal thing. You have to pick it yourself."

"Would you at least go with us?"

"And they cost too much anyway. A decent skateboard can cost a hundred bucks."

"She doesn't care."

"It's just not a good idea."

"But couldn't you just come with us?"

"No," I said. "And she shouldn't do it at all."

"Ohh-kay," said Macy. "Obviously someone's in a bit of a mood—"

"Why would someone think they could buy someone a skateboard?" I snapped. "It's idiotic."

I was driving too fast again. I made myself slow down.

Macy watched me. I could feel her eyes on me. "Are you okay?" she asked.

"I'm fine. Jesus."

She watched the houses going by on the right. "I heard about your parents."

"My parents are the least of my worries."

"Yeah? What is it, then? Is it something about Jennifer Hasselbach?"

"It's nothing," I said, lowering my voice. "I just didn't get enough sleep last night."

I didn't say anything more. We arrived at school.

I drove slowly over the speed bumps at the front entrance. "If you guys want to buy a skateboard, go to
that place at the mall."

"But that's why we wanted to ask you. Isn't there a
better place downtown? That's what everyone says."

"I don't know what's downtown," I lied, pulling
into a parking space. "I never go there."

"I thought you did. Everyone said you would
know."

"It's not true," I said. I turned off the car.

Macy unclicked her seat belt. "So you won't even
come?"

"No," I said. "And don't give me that look."

"What look?"

"Like I'm being an asshole about it."

"I'm not looking like that."

I got out and slammed my door. "You kinda are."

Macy got out and slammed hers. "Well you kinda
are being an asshole about it."

I walked away from her, toward the junior/senior
wing. It was so ridiculous about girls. They get these
schoolgirl crushes on you, and you can do no wrong.
Then they stop liking you and they want to boss you
around, like you were once their boyfriend, which you
never were. You never even liked them.

I went to class. I went to my locker. I went to the cafeteria for first lunch. Parker and James were sitting in
their usual spot, but Parker stood up the minute I sat
down. He had vocab to study. James left a few minutes
later.

So I ate by myself. I stabbed at my green beans with
my fork. I remembered freshman year when we'd kid
around and eat "prison-style." It was a game where
you kept your forearm in front of your tray, to guard
your food. Then the other guys tried to stab your fish
sticks, or sneak their hand under your armpit and steal
your Crunch bar or whatever. Just stupid frosh stuff.
Games you play. And now, here I was, barely able to eat
I was so scared. Eating "prison-style" wasn't so funny
anymore.

Macy and Rachel walked by; they had first lunch,
too. They sat at the end of my table with some other
sophomores. They talked for a minute, and then Rachel
came down the table to where I was.

"So Macy said you won't come downtown with us,"
she said, smiling, trying to put on the charm.

"I told her, you can't buy a guy a skateboard."

"Could you at least tell us where to go?"

"I don't know where to go. I told her to go to the mall."

"But there's a better place downtown. I know there is. Why won't you help us?"

"Because!" I said. "It's a bad idea!"

She became alarmed and went back to the other end of the table.

What the hell am I doing? I thought. *I've got to calm down.*

One thing I'd learned, though. When you think you're about to totally lose it, if you can just hang on a few more minutes, a few more seconds, things turn normal again.

That's what happened. I finished lunch and went to AP history. We watched the second half of *Doctor Zhivago*, and I sat in back and managed to sleep for almost an hour. That felt a lot better. Then for sixth period I had math, and Mr. Minter was in a good mood and gave everyone a "pass" grade on our last quiz because his computer screwed up.

I even felt bad about Macy and Rachel, and when I saw them after school, I yelled to them and waved them over to my car. I drew them a map to the skate shop downtown.

"But won't you come with us?" they pleaded. "We won't know which things are good."

I thought about it and realized if I didn't go with them I had nothing to do but worry and obsess all afternoon, so I said yes. We all got in my mom's car.

Downtown, we parked and walked to the skate shop. Rachel was serious about buying a skateboard. Her boyfriend was this boring guy named Dustin, who as far as I could tell never skated, or did much of anything. He sucked at basketball—I knew that because I'd seen him play rat-ball in the back parking lot.

Rachel studied all the decks carefully. She wanted to know about the different trucks and wheels and all that. It was kind of fun actually, playing Mr. Expert for an hour. I had bought my first board there. The board that was now under fifty feet of water in the Willamette River. As I looked at some of their new stuff, I regretted buying my new board at the mall. This place had the best stuff.

Rachel bought a board for $119. This seemed like too much to me. And the "anniversary," it turned out, was not for going out, but for the first time they talked on the phone or some ridiculous thing. Girls were so weird.

Once we had the board, we walked farther downtown and went to Starbucks. That was kinda fun. Rachel was pretty cool to hang out with. She was cute and funny, but in a real way. I wouldn't have minded going out with someone like her.

Macy was another story. She sort of bugged me for some reason. But my mood changed every three seconds. I couldn't tell what I thought.

After we'd sat there a few minutes, I glanced out the window. A girl caught my eye. She was across the street talking to a Streeter guy who was begging for change. The girl was sort of dirty, too. I couldn't see her face. Then she turned, and I saw who it was: Paisley.

I almost spit up my mocha. I lowered my head, but I realized she couldn't see through the window. She was busy talking anyway. The guy gave her a cigarette. She lit it and stood there smoking and talking to the guy.

"So have you bought Jennifer anything yet?" Rachel asked me. Macy had gone to the bathroom.

"Uh. No," I said. "Not yet."

She saw that I was looking outside. She looked, too, and saw Paisley and the guy with the dog. "Isn't it weird how kids like that live downtown? On the street?"

I nodded.

"I heard that there's more homeless teenagers in Portland than in any other city."

"Yeah?"

"Look at that girl," said Rachel. "She's probably younger than us. And she smokes. And dresses like that. Her parents probably hate her."

I turned away from the window. "So when are you going to give Dustin the board?" I asked.

"This weekend," said Rachel. "He'll be so psyched. Don't you think?"

"Yeah," I said. "It's a nice board."

I dropped Rachel off first. She got the board out of the backseat and skipped up her driveway with it. I felt this weird tingling in my heart. I had helped someone. I had done something worthwhile. It felt pretty good.

I drove Macy toward our street. We drove in silence. It started to rain, and I put on my windshield wipers.

"Can I ask you something?" asked Macy.

I didn't answer.

"You seem really weird lately," she said. "Are you okay?"

"I'm fine."

"I mean, your family stuff. That must be doing something to you. Don't you think?"

"I don't know."

"You seem so stressed. And when you're not freaking out, you have this look in your eyes. Like you're a thousand miles away."

I stared straight ahead. "Maybe it is my family stuff."

"Is it something about Jennifer?"

I shrugged. "I don't know, to be honest with you."

"You're not mad at *me* for some reason?"

"You?" I said. "No. Not at all."

"I don't have a crush on you anymore. If that's what you're worried about."

"I know."

"And I'm sorry, if I embarrassed you back then."

"It doesn't matter."

We drove.

"The whole thing with Jennifer . . ." she continued. "I have to say. That seems weird. She doesn't seem like your type. Like, I understand about Elizabeth and Christian, and how the other girls want skater boyfriends. But you and Jennifer. That just seems . . ."

"I know. I agree."

"Really? You don't really like her?"

"I like her. I mean, we had fun last summer. It's just like . . . she's just decided we should be together. She didn't let things develop naturally."

"That's it, isn't it? She's forcing things—"

"No, that's not it. To be honest."

"Really. What is it?"

I turned into our housing development. Windermeyer Terrace, it was called. Her house came up first. I pulled up to the curb in front of her house.

"It's just stuff that happened," I said.

"What stuff?" she asked, watching me. She meant it. She wanted to know.

"Just some things that happened," I said, quietly. "I can't really talk about it."

Something in my voice stunned her into silence. She could feel the weight of it now. She was shocked by the weight of it.

She blinked and stared at the dashboard. "Oh," she said. "It must be pretty bad."

"It's just one of those things."

She looked at me then. "Can I help you somehow?"

"I already feel a lot better," I managed to say. "Just saying anything at all."

"It must be bad."

"It's probably not what you think," I said. But then an alarm in my brain went off. I couldn't say any more about it. In fact, I may have already said too much. "It's really just stupid," I lied. "I mean, you know how it is. Sometimes you get all bent over nothing." I looked out my side window. "It's really nothing at all."

Macy didn't say anything.

"I gotta go," I said. "I gotta give my mom her car back."

Macy opened the door and got out. I pulled away and turned into my own driveway, six houses away.

◆▬◆▬◆▬◆▬◆▬◆▬◆▬◆▬◆

Two days later, I was sitting in math class when an announcement came over the intercom.

"Would the following people come to the principal's office. . . ." said the voice. I was one of the people. The others were Jared Fitch, Christian Barlow, Paul Auster, and a couple of the other known skaters.

I got up and walked to the front of the class. Everyone was, like, wow, all the cool skater guys are going to the principal's office.

I didn't feel very cool. I was scared to death. My legs felt like they might buckle at any moment.

I tried to clear my head as I walked the empty hallway. Behind me, Christian came out of biology. I waited for him. It reassured me to see him. He was one of the most popular boys at our school. Nothing bad could happen to him.

"What is this about?" he said when he saw me.

"Who knows."

"Probably going to complain about skating behind the cafeteria again," he said.

We walked together in silence to the principal's office. One of the other skaters appeared, a guy named Cal (for "California") who had also been summoned. He was very worried. He didn't do well with teachers, or authority, or anything, really.

We all went into the office. Mrs. Adams seemed a little on edge. The whole office seemed a little amped somehow. This wasn't a good sign. Jared came in. The other guys dribbled in. Paul Auster was chewing gum and was told to spit it out and got in an argument with Mrs. Adams. But something was up, something bigger than gum or skating behind the cafeteria.

When the seven of us were assembled, Mrs. Adams led us behind the counter and down the little hall. We passed the principal's office and arrived at a small conference room none of us had ever seen before. Inside, a man stood at a round table. He smiled at us pleasantly. He wore a sports coat and slacks. He had thick black hair, a thick neck, a thick head. In front of him was a briefcase and one of those little notebooks like reporters use. There was something hard in his face, though, something that gave me a chill down to my toes.

When we were all inside the room, he directed us to sit around the table. We each found a chair and sat.

Mrs. Adams told him he could have us as long as he wanted. He smiled and thanked her.

He closed the door and introduced himself. His name was Detective Matthew Brady. We could call him Matt. He was here investigating a murder that occurred downtown near a skatepark. The police department wanted to make some contacts within the skate community, in hopes of solving the case. He was visiting various high schools in the area and talking to skateboarders who might be able to help.

I didn't flinch. I didn't do anything. It was easy, with the other people there, to just sit and do nothing. Paul Auster looked guilty. So did Cal. Cal's face turned red.

"So first, let's go around and do names."

We did that. People told their names. People were scared, you could see it in their faces. You could hear it in their voices.

"So what exactly are you accusing us of?" said Paul, out of the blue.

"Nothing," said Detective Brady. "Nothing at all. None of you are suspects. What we're trying to do is get a better understanding of the skateboarding community."

"It's not a community," said Paul, irritably. "It's not like we know each other."

I was shocked he was talking like that to a police detective. He would make himself a suspect.

"No, I understand that," said Brady. "Let me give

you the background. We have a possible murder situation. The deceased was found on train tracks, just outside the central train yard downtown. Now the train
that was involved in the incident, before it gets to the
yard, passes near the Eastside Skatepark."

"*Paranoid* Park," said Paul. "Nobody calls it Eastside."

"Exactly," said the detective. "We think it's possible
that if this was a murder, someone from Paranoid Park
could be involved. The problem is, as we have discov-
ered, Paranoid Park is a unique place. There's a very
diverse group of people there, some of whom are hard
to track down. So we're trying to talk to people like
you guys, to see if we can better understand what goes
on there."

"You want names," said Paul Auster.

I couldn't believe he said that. Neither could Christian Barlow, who said, "Bro, he didn't say that, chill
out."

"Well," said Detective Brady, "I might need names
at some point. But what I need first is some background. . . . All right, who here has been to Eastside—
or, I mean, *Paranoid—*Park?"

At first I was afraid to raise my hand. But all
around me, hands went up. Mine went up, too, slowly,
cautiously.

"Great," said Detective Brady. "You all have. That's just what I was hoping for."

⊱⋅ ──────────── ⋅⊰

It was like a class, like a small AP class where everyone has to talk and the teacher expects you to have an opinion. Detective Brady did that on purpose, I suspected.

Actually, the situation was easy for me. I was one of the lesser skaters in the room, so it was totally natural for me to keep quiet. I sat, strangely calm, and watched the other guys talk about the various skateparks, the difference between "Streeters" and "Preps," etc. I tried to speak every once in a while. I would attempt to agree with something, and someone else would interrupt me. I managed somehow to believe the "part" I was playing: the clueless new guy who wanted to help, but didn't know much. It made perfect sense that I would mostly listen.

Then Detective Brady got more specific. Was anyone at Paranoid at any time during the weekend of September sixteenth and seventeenth?

Now, no hands went up. I looked over at Jared. He tentatively raised his hand.

"Yes, Jared?"

"We . . ." He pointed across the table at me. "We went, like, a week or two before that. During the day."

"What day?"

"I don't remember. Tuesday, maybe," said Jared. He was a little scared now. You could hear it in his voice. "And actually, we planned to go that weekend, but we didn't."

"Why didn't you?" said the detective. Suddenly he focused on me. He wanted me to talk.

"Uh . . ." I stammered. "Well, we . . . Jared . . . wanted to go down to Oregon State."

"So you did that instead?"

"I did," said Jared. "I went by myself. He stayed here."

"So *you* went to Paranoid?" said the detective, turning back to me.

I felt my face turn red. "No . . ." I said. "I . . . didn't want to go by myself."

"What did you do instead?"

"I . . . drove around for a while. And then I went home—"

"Paranoid isn't a place you want to go by yourself," interrupted Cal. "It's kinda dangerous."

"I go by myself," said Paul, defiantly. "People only mess with you there if you mess with them."

"I'm just saying," sputtered Cal. "It has a *reputation*."

"Were *you* there that weekend?" the detective asked Paul.

"Nah," Paul answered. "But I go there. I'm not afraid of it."

"Did anyone else go there, at any point during that week?"

No one had.

Detective Brady wrote this down. We talked some more, about other places people skate, which places had more Streeters, which places were more Prep.

After about forty minutes, Brady checked his watch. He had another high school to go to. He wrapped it up, giving each of us a business card and telling us if we heard anything to contact him.

"Skateboarders have a bad reputation in this city," he said. "You guys could do a lot to improve that if you could help us out."

Nobody seemed that enthusiastic. But Brady understood. He shut and locked his briefcase.

The meeting was over.

The seven of us headed straight for the restroom when we left the office. The bell was about to ring anyway; none of our teachers would expect us back.

We scattered around the boys' room. Jared sat in a sink, Christian leaned on the windowsill, Paul Auster sat on the heater by the door.

"What is up with that guy?" said Cal. "Why does he think *we* know something?"

"Who is he even talking about?" said Christian. "I didn't hear anything about a murder."

"I never saw a cop interview people in a group like that," said Paul Auster.

"That was seriously weird," I said.

"Why do they even leave Paranoid open?" said Cal. "It's so skanky."

"Because it's the best skatepark on the West Coast," said Jared. Everyone shut up for a minute. "And now they probably *will* close it. And nobody good will ever skate in Portland again."

"How do you figure it's the best skatepark?" asked Cal.

"Any idiot knows it's the best skatepark," answered Jared firmly. "It's been written up in every major skate magazine. Do you think Skate City has ever been in *Thrasher*?"

"There's chicks down there, too," added Paul.

"Yeah, *Streeter* chicks," said Christian. "With Streeter diseases."

"Hey, if you got a condom it doesn't matter."

"Unless it's crabs."

"Or scabies."

"Or lice."

"Dude, crabs *is* lice."

While the others talked, Jared turned to me. "So you didn't go down there that night?" he asked.

"No," I said, shaking my head.

"And you went home? I thought you went to my house?"

"I did . . . but I . . . that's what I meant. I went home to your house."

Jared accepted my explanation. "Pretty weird, though. We were almost there that night."

"Yeah, but it didn't happen at Paranoid. It happened at some train yard. It was, like, a half mile away."

"Huh," said Jared. "How do you know that?"

"That's what he just told us."

"When that skinhead got stabbed," Paul Auster told everyone, "his friends supposedly hunted down the guy and killed him and threw him in the river."

"That's stupid," said Cal. "He'd just float back up."

"Not if you put chains and cement around his ankles."

"Yeah, but eventually your ankles rot and your bones disconnect and the rest of you comes up to the surface."

"Or if they drag the river."

"Yeah, or if they dredge it, or whatever," said Cal.

"My brother knew this guy who used to do that. They'd find, like, cars and refrigerators and stuff. He said they found a leg once."

"Now I want to go check out Paranoid," said Paul. "See what's up. I wonder if everyone's freaking out."

"There's probably cops swarming all over down there."

"Maybe not," said Jared. "You saw that guy. It looks like they're trying a different approach. They're going for the psychological trap."

"Yeah, all that 'we want to better understand your community' crap. How stupid do they think we are?"

"Yeah, like cops ever trust skaters. *We want to help you with your reputation.* Sure, you do!"

"Yeah, how about that time you beat the crap out of those guys down at Suicide Stairwell for no reason? Were you helping us then?"

Everyone laughed. Paul Auster stuffed some gum in his mouth. "Frickin' cops."

⊷⊶⊷⊶⊷⊶⊷⊶⊷⊶⊷⊶⊷⊶

That night I went home and found my aunt Sally in my kitchen. "Your mother went to stay with your grand-mother tonight," she said. "She's upset and isn't feeling well."

I didn't see why we needed Aunt Sally around. It wasn't like we were totally helpless. At least she made brownies. That's what my aunt Sally always did when she got stressed.

Henry was sprawled in the living room, watching the big TV. I went upstairs to watch the news. I always watched the local news now, the long one at five thirty that had the most stuff on it.

I closed the door in the upstairs TV room. I turned on the TV and turned down the sound. The big story of the day was the new Trail Blazers coach. He was in trouble. He'd helped his players cheat in college and lied about some business deals. Now they were firing him. They showed him at a press conference lying about his lies.

Then the murder came up. They had a new graphic for it. Instead of the train tracks they'd been using, the little picture beside the woman's head now was a skateboard. Underneath, it said "Paranoid Park Murder." I crawled closer to the TV screen and turned up the volume slightly.

". . . Area police continue to focus on an unauthorized skatepark underneath the Eastside Bridge, known by locals as 'Paranoid Park.' The unsanctioned skatepark is about a quarter of a mile from where the body was found. Police say a community of homeless youth have been known to loiter in the area. . . ."

They had video footage from Paranoid. A guy with his shirt off did a front-side grind for the camera.

"Meanwhile, police continue to interview people here at the park, as well as local teenagers. . . ."

There was a short bit of video of a college girl who had obviously never been on a skateboard in her life. She had a tie-dyed shirt and a nose ring; she probably went to Reed. "Eastside Skatepark is part of this community," she said. "It's organic to its site, and we have to value that. . . ."

The newswoman added that the police still considered the incident a possible homicide.

The weather came on. I turned off the TV and went to my room. I had homework to do. I hadn't studied for anything in weeks. I couldn't let my grades completely nose-dive; it might arouse suspicion.

But I couldn't do homework. I opened the book, stared at it, but my brain wouldn't focus. So I lay on my bed and got out the card that Detective Brady gave each of us.

DETECTIVE MATTHEW BRADY
PORTLAND POLICE DEPARTMENT
HOMICIDE DIVISION

Along the bottom was a phone number and a Web site and an anonymous phone line to call in tips. I wondered if Jared would turn me in if he knew. I wondered if Scratch would turn me in. Maybe there was a reward. Would someone like Scratch turn me in for a couple hundred bucks? Probably. It didn't matter. They would catch me in the end. Or maybe they wouldn't. The world was so random. One of the things I'd seen on the Internet was that only a third of murder cases were ever solved. And this wasn't even necessarily a murder. It might still only be an accident.

———————

Detective Brady returned to our school a couple days later. An announcement from Mrs. Adams called Jared Fitch to the principal's office. I knew immediately it was Brady. From my science class I could see part of the faculty parking lot. I couldn't see a police car. He probably didn't have one anyway; he probably had an unmarked. I still knew it was him.

I sat in my class. I could feel the pressure of Detective Brady on the school grounds. Would he call us in one at a time? Probably. Adults loved the one-at-a-time approach. Maybe he just wanted information. It made sense. Who would know about Paranoid Park better than skaters? Or maybe they got Scratch and he confessed and told them the murderer was a Prep, a nice kid from the suburbs. And now they were hunting that person down.

I stared out the window. I imagined riding to the police station, my hands cuffed behind my back. That would be fine with me. It really would. I was done. There was no point now. My life sucked so much, I might as well get caught.

I smiled as I thought that. I almost started to laugh. A week before, I had been so scared I was pissing myself. Now, with a homicide detective a few hundred feet down the hall, I was thinking, *What are we having for lunch today? I wonder if Dustin liked his board? I wonder how many years I'll get in prison?* I was like, dude, whatever. I didn't care. I was sick of worrying about it. Whatever happened, happened. *Go ahead, Brady,* I thought. *Bring it on.*

The bell rang. I walked to Jared's locker to see what was up. He wasn't there. I saw Cal in the hall. He grabbed my arm. "Is that detective guy here? Is he gonna call us all in?"

"How would I know?" I said.

"Man, I hate things like this."

"What do you care? You didn't do anything."

"I know," he said. "But I hate cops."

"When have you ever dealt with cops?"

"I dunno. You know what I mean."

I walked away. I went to my next class. And then about halfway through it, there was a new announcement. It was me this time. My name. My name and no others.

I was to report to the principal's office. Now.

⭒⭒⭒⭒⭒⭒⭒⭒⭒⭒⭒⭒⭒⭒⭒

I walked slowly, calmly through the empty hallway. I felt proud of myself in a way. I was handling this. I was dealing with it.

In my mind, I rehearsed my story. We had planned to go to Paranoid, then Jared bailed to party with the girl at Oregon State and I drove around. I went back to Jared's and spent the night. Then I went home the next morning.

That was my story and I'd stick to it. If they busted me, they busted me.

I walked into the office. Mrs. Adams led me around the counter, through the hall, and into the same room we'd been in before.

Detective Brady sat reading some papers, making notes. He sipped a cup of Dunkin' Donuts coffee. I watched him more closely than at the first meeting. He looked tired today. I wondered how old he was. Thirty?

Thirty-five? I also noticed he had a redneck haircut—
no sideburns, too short on top. He was probably from
the East Side himself.

"Hello there," he said.

"Hi."

"Have a seat."

I did. He told me he was talking to everyone indi-
vidually. He wanted to make sure he had his paperwork
together. He went through my info, checking my name,
my address, my age. It was all the same as before.

"Sorry to take you out of class."

"That's okay," I said.

"So. Anyway. I talked to Jared and he says you almost went to the Eastside Skatepark the night of the
seventeenth. Is that right?"

"Yes," I said. I suddenly felt dryness in my throat.
I tried to remember how freaked out Cal was. Even
someone who was perfectly innocent would feel nervous talking to a homicide detective. So I was fine. I
was a little nervous, but that was natural.

"So you . . . drove around that night?"

"Yes. I . . . well . . . we went there another time and I
was . . . well, I thought it was cool and everything, but
it was pretty hard-core. I'm not that good of a skater,
so I didn't want to go there by myself."

"Did you drive by there that night?"

"No."

"Where did you go?"

"That night? I . . . I drove around . . . downtown a little. And since I was downtown anyway, I got something to eat. And I . . . then I parked down near the waterfront. And walked around a little."

"Were you skateboarding?"

"Yeah. Well, actually, no, not really that night. I mean, I had my skateboard. Like I said, I'm not as good as the other guys. So I try to practice by myself."

Detective Brady nodded. "So can you give me some times for these things? Approximately?"

"Uh . . . I went to Jared's around seven or eight. Then we went to the bus station a little after that. And then I drove around. And then . . . oh, yeah . . . that was something I got confused about before. I didn't go home. I went to Jared's. Because we had originally planned to sleep over at his house that night."

"Where were his parents?"

"His mom was in Las Vegas. His dad doesn't live with them."

"No brothers or sisters? The house was totally empty?"

"Right," I said. "His sister lives in Seattle." I swallowed dryly.

"And did your parents know this? That no one was home at Jared's?"

"Uh . . ."

Brady made a note. "So this is the old trick where you tell your parents you're sleeping at Jared's and your parents don't realize his parents are gone, and then you can do whatever you want?"

"Uh . . . well . . ."

"No, I understand," he said, smiling slightly. "We used to do that. It's an old one."

"Yeah, I guess so."

Brady studied me. "So what's *your* parental situation?"

"Uh . . . what do you mean?"

"Your parents, they're together?"

"No. They're separated. Or they're . . . well, they'll probably get divorced."

Detective Brady nodded. A thoughtful look came over his face. "My parents got divorced. When I was about your age, actually. That's a tough thing to go through."

"Yeah," I said.

"Do you have brothers and sisters?"

"A brother. Younger. He's thirteen."

"Do you have a sister?"

"No."

"How about a girlfriend?"

"Uh . . . yeah, sort of."

"Where was she that night?"

"She was with her other friends."

"Did you call her at any point? Do you have a cell phone?"

"No. I didn't call her. We just started going out, actually."

"So she wasn't your girlfriend a couple weeks ago?"

"Right. I mean, we weren't totally hanging out yet. She's more of a girlfriend now."

"How's that going?"

"What?"

"Having a girlfriend."

I shrugged. "It's good, I guess."

"You sound unsure," said Detective Brady, smiling slightly.

"No, it's okay. She's kinda . . . I don't know. We just started going out. It hasn't really solidified."

"I see."

"But it's okay. I mean, she's nice."

Detective Brady smiled and nodded. He tapped the point of his pen on the paper in front of him. "So, getting back to this . . ." he said. "I'm trying to think about this situation. This security guard. We find him, you know, deceased on these train tracks. We think, okay, he tripped, he fell. But then the autopsy says he was hit with a blunt object."

I nodded.

"My boss has this idea that some kids might have been riding that train, just for fun, which apparently happens a lot. They're riding along, the security guard sees them, and he tries to kick them off. There's some sort of confrontation, maybe a struggle, the guy ends up dead, and the kids take off."

I tried to look slightly confused.

"So what I'm trying to imagine is," continued Brady, "what do these kids do then? Where do they go? What kind of kids are they?"

I swallowed. "Yeah, that's a good question."

"What would you do? If you were one of those kids."

"I . . . I don't know. Call the police?"

"What if the other kids were your friends? Would you call the police on your friends?"

"I think I would if someone got killed. Or if it was an accident or whatever."

Detective Brady thought about my answer. "What if you were alone? What if you were by yourself and something like this happened?"

I looked into my lap. "Then I'd definitely call the police. Because, why not? Unless you wanted to kill the guy. I mean, myself, I don't have anything against security guards."

"Right. But what would you do if you didn't call the police?" said Brady, with a new energy in his voice. "Like, what if you got scared and you didn't know what to do?"

I glanced up at him then, thinking he would be staring at me, staring at me hard, coming in for the kill. But he wasn't. He was focused on the pen in his hand. He was deep in thought.

"I'm not sure," I said.

"You'd run probably," said Detective Brady. "And you'd go back to the skatepark and tell your friends. Or if you were smart, you wouldn't go back to the skatepark; you'd head for the river and hope nobody saw you."

"Yeah . . . I guess so."

"And these kids," continued Brady, "they're probably transients. Or runaways. They're probably in trouble already. If I was them, I think I'd hop the first train out of town. Get out of the state. Out of the country, even. . . ."

I swallowed. "I heard someone got stabbed there once . . ." I said.

"Do you know any street kids? I mean, yourself personally."

"No," I said. "I mean, I've seen them. 'Streeters,' people call them. Some of them skate. Most of them just beg for change and stuff."

"If I showed you photos, could you pick out people you've seen in the area?"

I shrugged cautiously. "I doubt it. It's not like I know any of them."

Brady thought about this for a long time. Then he checked his watch. "All right," he said. "I'm going to have to cut this short."

I said nothing.

He packed up his briefcase and got out another business card. I noticed his hands as he handed it to me. They were big and thick, meaty-looking. He wore one of those big rings, like car salesmen wear in movies.

I tried my best to look meek and confused. "So I can go back to class?"

"Yeah. Hey, and thanks. I appreciate it." He leaned over the table and offered me that same thick hand. I shook it.

Then I got the hell out of there.

Dear ____,

I hadn't seen much of Jennifer during this time. She made varsity cheerleader for basketball, so that week she was practicing every day after school. Then Elizabeth and some of her friends went ice-skating on Saturday, and Jennifer wanted me to come.

A bunch of people went. Christian was there, and a couple other boyfriends. We all sat at a picnic table drinking hot chocolate, and Christian told the girls about our meeting with Detective Brady. It was weird because he told the story like I hadn't even been there. The whole group of them talked about this thing that *I* did, this whole situation that *I* caused, but since everyone looked up to Christian so much, nobody could imagine I had anything to do with it. They only wanted to listen to him. Even when he told everyone I had been interviewed, too, the girls were like, whatever, and wanted to hear more about him. Which was fine with me. Sometimes it was good to be a wallflower.

After ice-skating, we all went to Elizabeth Gould's house. She had this fancy hot tub, and everybody stripped to their underwear and sat in it and looked at the stars.

Even though it was fun, I kept thinking of Detective Brady. As we got dressed again, I asked Christian, "Do you think Brady knows more than he's telling us?"

"Like what?"

"Like maybe he knows something and he's playing dumb. Like he's trying to trick us."

"I doubt it."

"The whole thing is pretty weird, though," I said. "A detective showing up at school. Talking to skate-boarders."

Christian scoffed. "Cops are stupid. Why do you think they're cops? Do you know how much money they make? Like, the same as a janitor."

"Yeah," I said. "But maybe they do it for other reasons."

"Dude, grown-ups do stuff for money," said Christian, tightening his belt. "There are no other reasons."

Afterward, I went back to Jennifer's house. She was acting all sexy, and we went straight to her bedroom to make out. But I couldn't stay focused.

"What is wrong with you tonight?" she said, pulling away.

"Nothing."

"You're acting so . . . out of it."

"How am I supposed to act?"

"I dunno. But you could say something every once in a while. Christian and Elizabeth talk. They have a relationship."

I stared at her. "What does that mean?"

"When Christian says something, he says it. When you say something, people interrupt you. And you let them."

I stood up. "I'm sorry if I'm not Mr. Popular, like Christian."

"I'm just saying, you could be a better boyfriend," she said. She got up and tucked her shirt in.

I didn't know what to say. She was probably right.

"You better go; my parents will be home soon," she said.

"Can you give me a ride home?"

"That's another thing," complained Jennifer. "You need to get your own car. You can't just skateboard everywhere."

But that's what I did. I skateboarded home from her house. In the rain. In the dark. I was glad to do it. I was glad to be on my own.

That night I had a dream about Detective Brady. I dreamed that he came to live with my brother and me. He was a relative of ours, it turned out. I sat with him at the airport, and he told me about his parents' divorce—how it made him become a cop. He said all cops' parents were divorced; it was one of the requirements.

Then the dream changed, and I was at school and people were congratulating me. Everyone was really impressed about something I did. I felt accepted and comfortable and like everything was all right again.

Unfortunately, when I woke up I was back in reality. Nobody was happy about anything, least of all me. At least it was Sunday. I got up and went downstairs. I ate breakfast and then Jared called. Did I want to come skate with him and Paul Auster and check out the new rails at the convention center? I did.

Jared picked me up. When I got in the car, he looked at my board. "That isn't your board."

"Yeah it is, I just got it."

"What'd you get a new board for?"

"My dad bought it for me," I said, which was sort of true. "I wanted to try something different."

Jared looked at it. "Why didn't you tell me?"

"Why would I tell you?" I said, grabbing it back from him.

"I gotta skate with you, dude. I don't want some wuss board riding next to me."

"It's not a wuss board. It's better than your lame board."

We picked up Paul Auster. We drove downtown. I worried they might change their mind and want to go to Paranoid Park. But they didn't. They wanted to check out the new stairs and rails at the convention center.

The new rails were popular that day. All the local skaters had heard about them, and a lot of the best guys had shown up to try them out.

I couldn't ride rails. Neither could any of us, really. Jared tried and just about killed himself. I mostly hung out and messed around on a three-set on the other end of the plaza, but after I crashed a couple times I laid off that, too.

Paul Auster and I ended up sitting together, drinking Red Bulls and watching this Prep kid do tricks on the sidewalk. He was this dorky kid, but he was nailing kick-flips, manuals, shuv-its, everything. He was a natural talent; he didn't *try* to do things, he just did them. There was no thinking.

I drank my Red Bull and reflected on that. Before the security guard, almost everything I did was natural. I woke up, I went to school, I hung out with my friends. I never thought about what I was doing, or why. Now I was always thinking. I never just *did* stuff. I was always checking myself, watching what I said and did. Which made every day like going to work. It was like my whole life had become a really hard job.

But what exactly caused that? And how did you fix it? Could you go back to being innocent and carefree once you'd done something like what I did?

I didn't know. And there was no one to ask.

That night my mom came home. My aunt Sally packed her stuff to go. They were both pretty stressed. My mom especially. She took some sleeping pills and went to bed.

Henry and I watched TV until eleven and then he went to bed. I watched the news. I always watched the news. I knew everything going on in the whole state. But there was nothing about Paranoid Park.

Later, I went to the garage. I wanted to see what

camping stuff my dad had taken. The little camp stove was gone, of course. But the bigger stove was still there. The cooler was still there. I tried to find the emergency crank-up radio my mom gave Dad as a Christmas gift, but he must have taken it.

I looked through the other cabinets. The sleeping bags were still there—the older ones, anyway. I found a little cot that folded up and fit into a carrying bag. I pulled it out and tried to remember how to set it up. The instructions were gone, but once I unfolded it, I figured it out.

I thought about if I had to run. Like if the cops began to figure things out, could I get away? Where would I go?

I could probably make it to Canada. If I left in the morning. I could pretend I was going to school, take my mom's car, and be in Vancouver, B.C., by nightfall.

Then what? Live in a stolen car? How long would that last? Maybe I could go to Mexico. That was farther. Two days' drive, maybe three. I could say I was staying over at Jared's. That would give me a day. And if I drove all night, I could probably make it. But what would I do in Mexico? What would I do anywhere?

I folded up the cot. I dug around some more. I found a little survival kit that had a compass and aspirin and some waterproof matches. I found a little bottle of antidote for rattlesnake bites. I wondered what that did to you.

Maybe I could take some of my mom's sleeping pills. If I tried to kill myself, would they go easy on me? Could I say I was insane or suicidal or whatever?

I dug deeper in one of the standing cabinets. I found some snowshoes that my dad bought. A couple years before, he decided he was "into" snow camping. He never actually went, but he bought all the crap. Most of it was useless, but the snowshoes were kinda cool.

I found some fishing stuff, some old reels, some old tackle boxes. I opened a coffee can and found a tangle of hooks and bobbers and other stuff. When I was a little kid, I used to dream of going into the mountains and living off the land. I guess a lot of kids think that. Hunting for food, using a bow and arrow, living in a tree house or in a cave . . . But that's not what it would be like if I bailed. It wouldn't be a Disney movie. Running away would be a slow, dirty, gruesome existence. Hiding out, sleeping in the car—what would I do for money? I could get dishwashing jobs. Maybe I could meet a girl somewhere, a Canadian girl. I could live behind her house and we could get married and change our names and . . . . I don't know what . . . grow vegetables, listen to Bright Eyes, hang out in hammocks. . . .

It was a nice dream. There were a lot of nice dreams.

But could I do it? Maybe it was better to just go to jail, just do my time and not cut ties. Better to have my dumb parents know where I was than be out in the Canadian wilderness somewhere, alone, eating dirt, slowly going insane. . . .

That was the thing about secrets, they drove you insane. They really did. They isolated you. They separated you from your tribe. They destroyed you eventually. Unless you were strong. Unless you were very, very strong.

I found Jennifer in the parking lot after school a couple days later. She was wearing her cheerleader uniform. She stood with Elizabeth and those guys by Elizabeth's car.

Jennifer had told me earlier that she was going with Elizabeth Gould that weekend to the Goulds' beach house with some other girls. She wanted me to be jealous about their "girls' party weekend" or whatever, but I wasn't.

I walked over to them. I had my skateboard under my arm. None of them looked very happy to see me. I was not being a good boyfriend to Jennifer. I had not turned out to be the fun-loving skater boy they thought I would be.

"Hey," I said to Jennifer. "Can I talk to you a second?"

She gave me a harsh look, for her friends' benefit. But she came. She seemed a little curious about what I wanted.

"I can't go out with you anymore," I told her.

"What?!" she said. She was totally shocked. She thought I had come to complain about her going to the beach. "What are you talking about?"

"I don't think it's working out," I said.

"What? Are you serious? Who have you been talking to?"

"No one."

"Oh my God!" She looked at me, her mouth open. She was so surprised she couldn't think of what to say.

"You can't break up with me," she finally blurted. "We just started going out!"

"I know. I'm sorry. But I don't think it's working out."

"Why did you wait until now?" she said. "Were you waiting until you had sex with me?"

"No. I just . . ."

"You were! You waited until you had sex with me! You used me!"

"No, I didn't."

She hit me. A slapping blow to my upper arm. I stepped away from her.

"I just don't feel like it's—" I repeated.

"I can't believe you!" she shrieked, louder now, so her friends would hear. "You think you can just dump me? Now that we've had sex? You can't do that."

I stood there, watching her. The whole world was a dream, I realized. Nothing was real. Everyone was acting in a bad soap opera. The whole world was one big FOX TV show.

"Jennifer?" asked one of the other cheerleaders. "Are you okay?"

Jennifer ran to her friends. "He just broke up with me!" She burst into tears. She ran to Elizabeth, who put her arms around her.

All the girls stared at me with hatred in their eyes. It was a big drama that had to be acted out. But deep down, nobody really cared. The other girls didn't care about Jennifer. Jennifer didn't care about me. I didn't care about anything.

Everyone was so full of crap.

<hr />

The next day, the news went around school: I had used Jennifer for sex and dumped her. I didn't try to defend myself. There was no point.

I found Christian and those guys skating behind

the cafeteria after school and they asked me about it. What was my plan? Did I like someone else? Why had I given up free sex?

"She was hot," said Paul. "I hope you have some sort of backup."

"She was too social," I said. "Everything was a little drama for her and her friends."

Paul thought I was crazy. Christian didn't care either way. Only Jared understood. He never liked her that much but had encouraged me anyway, under the principle that getting laid was always better than not getting laid.

Later, I took the bus home. Skating down my street, I saw a strange car parked at the curb outside my house. It was a navy-blue American car, with thick black tires. I skated right up to it and saw—too late—that it was Detective Brady. He sat in the driver's seat, writing something.

"Hey there," he said when he saw me.

"Oh, hi," I answered.

"Hey, I was wondering. I got an hour. I wanted to drive downtown and just sort of . . . poke around. Check out the kids. Wanna come?"

"Uh. I probably shouldn't. . . . I have homework."

"We'll keep it short. A half hour."

"But my mom—"

"Your mom's not home. And she won't care. You're helping with police business."

"I really—"

"Come on, get in."

I didn't seem to have a choice. I got in.

⊱⊱⊱⊱⊱⊱⊱⊱⊱⊱⊱⊰⊰

"How's school?" Brady asked me, after we'd driven in silence for a few minutes.

"Okay," I answered. I didn't like being in his car. It was too personal. And it was kinda trashed. There were papers and folders everywhere, and McDonald's bags and old Dunkin' Donuts coffee cups down by my feet.

"High school," said Brady, smiling to himself. "It didn't seem like much at the time. But you think back— the parties, the girls, the football games. . . ."

I stared out the window. "I actually just broke up with my girlfriend," I said.

"Oh, yeah? What happened?"

"Nothing. I just broke it off."

"How come?"

"Just not into it."

"Any particular reason?"

I shrugged. "It didn't seem right. I didn't really like her. She didn't really like me."

"Yeah, well. You can't fool people. Sooner or later the truth comes out."

I didn't like the sound of that. I watched out the window as we entered downtown. It was weird being in that car. I didn't like it, but on the other hand I felt protected somehow. And it seemed like my story was working, that I was the innocent kid who had done nothing wrong, who had never been to Paranoid Park, except one time, during the day, with Jared.

I also felt like . . . well . . . I sorta *liked* Brady for some reason. I mean, I was terrified of him, naturally. But being near him seemed safer than not being around him, and not knowing what he was doing, or thinking.

And another thing: He seemed different from other people. He was a cop. He'd seen stuff. He'd dealt with the brutal realities of life. Not like most people. Most people never dealt with anything. A divorce maybe, at the most. But what was a divorce? It was nothing.

Brady knew that. So did I.

"You ever seen this girl?" said Brady. He handed me a picture of a young girl. She looked homeless and drugged out.

"No," I said. "What did she do?"

"Nothing. She's a runaway."

"I thought you only did homicides?"

"I do."

I wasn't sure what that meant, so I shut up. I watched the people on the street as we drove around more. Because he was a cop, Detective Brady could drive anywhere he wanted. He pulled onto River Walk and drove on the bike path. We moved slowly through the bikeriders and joggers. People would get pissed at a car being there, until they looked in the car and saw Brady's face. Then they turned around and minded their own business.

At the far end of River Walk, we saw some skaters under the Morrison Bridge.

"Never could do anything with a skateboard," said Detective Brady, slowing down.

"They had them back then?"

He smiled. "I'm not *that* old."

We cruised slowly past the skaters. "You recognize any of these people?"

"Where would I recognize them from?" I said.

"From anywhere," said Detective Brady.

I shook my head. "Never seen them before."

"So this girl," said Detective Brady, turning the car around. "The one you broke up with. What was her deal?"

I stared out the window. "I dunno. She thought she was supposed to have a boyfriend. So she got one. But she didn't even know me."

"It's always so interesting," said Detective Brady, "how people do what they think they're supposed to. We're not nearly as independent as we think. You learn that being a cop. I'd like to say we catch every criminal with our brilliant crime-solving techniques, but the truth is, most of them come to us. That social instinct kicks in—the guilt, it wears them down."

"Huh," I said, casually.

"There are exceptions. Sociopaths. They don't have that guilt mechanism. They don't feel it in their gut. Or young kids, gang members, they think of themselves as soldiers. That seems to insulate them psychologically. Or else they're on some ego trip. They think they're God, or above other people in some way. But those are the exceptions. Most murderers are loose nuts. If they had any self-control, they'd never have committed the crime in the first place."

As he said this, Detective Brady steered his car along a different bike path. I soon saw why: Ahead of us, a group of street kids were sitting around a fountain. There were about eight of them. They were real Streeters: dirty, homeless. "You recognize any of these guys?" he said.

"I really don't know any of these people," I said, annoyed that he kept asking me. "I don't hang out down here."

But even as I spoke, I saw I was wrong. I did know one of them. Paisley. She sat on the end of the bench, eating a candy bar. My heart thudded in my chest. I looked away, kept my eyes down, and prayed she wouldn't look at the car.

She didn't. She looked at her candy bar and the girl sitting next to her. Detective Brady gave them a long look. But he kept driving.

I took a long silent breath, and then Paisley was behind us and I was safe inside my innocent-kid story again.

⟡⟡⟡⟡⟡⟡⟡⟡⟡⟡⟡⟡⟡⟡⟡

Meanwhile, normal life went on. It was autumn now—the leaves were changing, pumpkins appeared in front windows, people began wearing sweaters and track jackets. The football team had won a couple games and people got psyched about that. Homecoming and Halloween were right around the corner. Everyone seemed happy and excited and hopeful. . . .

But not me. I was in social freefall. I was now totally scorned by the Jennifer/Elizabeth crowd, which meant Christian Barlow and Paul Auster couldn't hang out with me as much. Jared was chasing one of Jennifer's friends, so it put him in a difficult situation. They kinda had to cut me loose. To be honest, I was glad. It was too hard trying to act normal all the time. Though when Friday and Saturday nights came and I had nothing to do, that sucked.

At least I could skate. But that got harder, too. It started raining again, and the only decent indoor place was Skate City at the mall, which was full of twelve-year-olds. Skating in the rain was better than that place.

⊶⊷⊶⊷⊶⊷⊶⊷⊶⊷⊶⊷⊶⊷⊶

And then my parents' divorce proceedings officially started. My mom totally lost it. She took sleeping pills every night and went to bed right after dinner, some-times before. Or she'd go stay at Grandma's and Aunt Sally would come over. Aunt Sally didn't have kids, so she had all these weird rules that didn't make sense. And she was a vegetarian, too, so the dinners she made were pretty gross. The brownies were good, though.

The first envelopes from the lawyers started com-ing to the house. Henry and I would see them in the mail slot. I found myself wishing I could talk to Detective

Brady about it. I wondered what advice he would have. He was one of the few people in the world I might listen to.

But mostly I just felt numb. I woke up every day and put on my clothes and went to school. My grades began to slide, and I barely talked to anyone. You'd think a teacher or someone would have said something, but they didn't. They probably figured it was the divorce.

I was also not as scared anymore. I stopped worrying that I would suddenly get caught. I read on the Internet that if they didn't solve a murder case in the first two weeks, the chances of ever solving it were, like, three percent.

I tried to do homework. About once a week or so, I would study for a couple hours and actually remember what I studied. But most nights I would zone out. I'd sit in front of the TV and go catatonic. I didn't feel happy, I didn't feel sad; I just felt sick. I felt like I would *get* sick. I was pretty sure I'd eventually get cancer.

But then other times, driving my mom's car or sitting in class, I'd think, *At least I'm free. At least I can skate when I want. There's no court date, no lawyers, my fate isn't in the hands of anyone but myself.*

But was that really freedom? When there was all this dark stuff in my brain, all these things I could

never speak of, or tell anyone about. Any place could
be a prison, I realized, if your head wasn't right.

Even a nice house in the suburbs.

Around the end of October, I started skating Vista
again. Vista was an old, winding street that traversed
the West Hills and eventually led downtown. There
were different side streets you could take. Younger
skaters and beginners liked it; it was about two miles
of easy cruising. At the bottom, you could get the city
bus back to the top for a buck fifty. Sometimes you
could slip in the back door and not pay at all.

Anyway, I got in the habit of doing that on nights
when I couldn't stand to be home and couldn't think
of anything else to do. I would stay out for hours. You
could even do it in the rain. It was pretty chill, slalom-
ing the smooth streets, with an iPod or whatever, the
wet night air misting your face. . . .

One night I was doing that, cruising Vista. A light
rain fell. No one was out—a few cars, no people. The
streets were wet and I got going a little too fast, and
when I hit the bus stop at the bottom, I couldn't make
the turn back up the hill. So I bombed the rest of it,
and went downtown. I wanted a coffee anyway, and I

was getting cold. I kept my speed up and cruised the Twenty-First Street strip, which is where I saw Macy.

She was standing outside the Saigon Café. She was talking to Rachel and Rachel's boyfriend Dustin. I would have kept going, but she saw me and yelled my name. So I stopped, which screwed up my plan to make it all the way to the train station. But that was okay. I hadn't had the best luck with trains lately.

Rachel and Dustin were going home. Dustin didn't have the board Rachel bought him, but he said how awesome it was and thanked me and babbled on about how he was learning to ollie. Obviously, if he was truly into it, he'd have his board with him, but whatever— not everyone is born to skate.

Rachel and Dustin offered us a ride home. I said I was good, that I wanted to get a coffee, and then Macy said she wanted to stay, too, and we would take the bus back. I didn't think that was necessary—her hanging out—but truthfully, I was glad. I needed the company.

We got coffees and sat outside, beneath the awnings at Saigon. It was still misting out, so it was fun to drink hot coffee while the rain fell quietly on the street.

"So how are things with your parents?" Macy asked me. Obviously the neighbors had been discussing the plight of my loser family.

"Not that good. It's official now. They're getting divorced."

"That must be hard."

"Maybe it's good. At least it's out in the open. At least everyone knows what's happening."

"Where's your dad?"

"Staying with my uncle."

Macy sipped her coffee. We both sat with our backs to the café, staring at the wet street. I pulled a chair around so we could put our feet up. She liked that. She put her dainty Pumas up next to my huge, dirty skate shoes. Our feet looked like Beauty and the Beast.

"So does Rachel's boyfriend ever use his new skateboard?" I asked.

"Not really," she said. "But he still likes it. It's the thought that counts."

I nodded. A car drove by, its wheels *whooshing* on the wet pavement. I snuggled deeper into my coat and stared at my feet.

"So I heard about you and Jennifer," said Macy.

"Yeah."

"That didn't last very long."

"No," I said.

"Why did you break up with her?"

"Why was I going out with her? Who knows?"

"You must have liked her a little."

"I liked her last summer. Before she decided I was her boyfriend."

"With all the stuff you're going through, I guess something like that would be hard. . . ."

I laughed at that and sipped my coffee.

"Why do you laugh?" said Macy.

"All the things I'm *going through*," I said. "It sounds so ridiculous."

"But you're going through a lot," she said seriously.

I tried to shrug it off, but the way she said that got to me. *Sympathy.* I needed it. I was starved for it. I was so grateful for it, I felt tears come into my eyes.

But I held them back. "Lots of people's parents get divorced," I said. "There are worse problems."

"Like what?"

"People getting killed in Iraq. Little kids starving in Africa."

Macy looked at me. "Since when are you worried about starving children in Africa?"

"You know what I mean. Our little problems. Our little *issues*. It's all so stupid."

"Not if it's happening to you."

"Bigger stuff can happen to people than their parents splitting up."

"Yeah? Like what?"

"Like stuff."

She stared into the street. "Did something happen to you?" she said quietly.

"No. I just mean in general."

"What happened to you?"

"Nothing. You know what I mean."

Macy sipped her coffee. That was the thing about Macy. She wasn't the dumb girl from down the street anymore. When she asked you something, the question sunk into you. You had to answer.

"No," I said. "I just feel like there are other things that happen. Outside normal life. Outside parents and girlfriends and breakups. Like right out there." I pointed into the dark street. "There are other levels of things."

Macy was unsure of what I was talking about.

"Something *did* happen to me," I said, before I could stop myself.

But Macy proved just how cool she was at that moment. She didn't ask me what. She didn't say anything. She just sat there, with her coffee, staring into the darkness. If I wanted to say more I could. If I didn't . . . well, that was okay, too. . . .

Macy and I rode the bus home. We sat side by side, our hips touching, our elbows knocking occasionally. I held my skateboard between my legs and spun one of the wheels with my fingers.

An old man got on at Burnside. A woman with a PBS book bag dropped her change in the slot. I could smell Macy; her thick hair had frizzed out slightly in the rain. We rode up the hill. I pointed out the place where you caught the bus at the bottom of Vista. I pointed out some of the good skateboarding streets.

Macy's cell phone rang. It was her mom. They had a short fight about when she was coming home. Macy didn't back down at all. I didn't remember her being so defiant to her parents. I found myself watching her talk, watching her face.

Also, she had a body. I hadn't really noticed that before. She wore a tight sweater under her coat, and I could see it as she talked. Not that I was thinking about that. It was just more evidence of the transformation of Macy.

She hung up and tucked her cell phone away. We rode for a while in silence. "So Rachel and Dustin seem pretty happy together," I said.

"Yeah."

"What about you?" I asked. "Do you like any boys?"

"Where did that come from?" she asked.

"You asked me about Jennifer."

"It's not really the same," she said.

"Do you want a boyfriend?"

"I would if I liked someone. And if they liked me."

"Jennifer was insane about having a boyfriend," I said, spinning my wheel. "She'll have a new one by the end of next week."

Macy didn't answer. She stared out the rainy window. "What happened to you?"

"What do you mean?"

"You said something happened to you."

"Just this thing happened. I can't talk about it, really."

"What kind of thing?"

"It was nothing, really."

"It didn't sound like nothing."

"It's nothing."

"All right. If you say so," she said. Her phone rang again. She checked to see who it was, then put it away.

"Have you ever had something happen . . . ?" I found myself saying. "Something that really eats at you, but you can't really talk about?"

"Yeah. I guess so."

"What did you do?" I asked. "How did you forget about it?"

"Time makes you forget eventually."

"Time heals all wounds?"

"Yeah. Or you tell someone," she said. "You don't want to keep certain things secret. Or it'll build up inside you."

"I know. But what if you *can't* tell anyone?"

"Like what? Like if you got molested or something? You're supposed to tell stuff like that. That's exactly what you should tell."

"No, but what if it's something like, not in my case, but if you were in a war or something. And you saw horrible things."

"You go to a shrink. Because then you'll get that post-traumatic thing."

I worried I had given away too much. I needed to say something to throw her off. "Or what if you took something? And you didn't think it was that valuable, but then it turns out it is."

Macy shrugged. "I don't know. Try to give it back?"

"What if you can't?"

"Then you just . . . try to pay them back in some other way. Or just let it go if there's nothing you can do."

I spun the wheels of my skateboard with my hand.

We arrived at our stop. I pushed the button and we got off the bus. We walked down the street together. Dark clouds moved silently across the sky.

"You do seem different lately," said Macy.

"So do you," I said.

"I do? How do I seem different?"

"You're showing up at parties. You're hanging out. You're wearing Pumas."

"I always wore Pumas."

"You used to be a nerd," I said.

"You just think that because I liked you."

"You *were* a nerd. Riding around on your little bike. With the little training wheels."

"I did training wheels when I was six. Everyone does training wheels."

"You know what I mean."

We had arrived at her house. We both stood for a minute in the street at the bottom of her driveway.

"Well, I'm still sorry about your parents and all that," she told me.

"Yeah, thanks," I said.

"And whatever other dark secrets you've got in there," she said, smiling and sticking her finger into my temple like a gun.

"I don't really have any secrets," I said, trying to joke around.

"Yes you do," she said.

I didn't answer. I gripped my skateboard. Above

us, the towering evergreen trees swayed in the wind.
For a moment I had a strange thought. That Macy and
I . . . that we could . . .

"All right," she said. "I better go. Or my stupid
mom's gonna call me again."

"Okay."

"Thanks for the coffee," said Macy.

"No problem," I said.

Dear ____,

By November, there were no more mentions of the Paranoid Park murder. It was never on TV or in the paper. New murders had replaced it, new crimes, and of course the papers were always full of news about the Portland Trail Blazers. They had fired the new coach and gotten a newer one, who had "better values" and who would better represent our community—whatever that meant.

On the two-month anniversary of September seventeenth, I skated Vista. I had hoped there would be a sense of relief by now. I wanted to think if I could hold on, if I could keep going, I would eventually pass through to a better place. But there didn't seem to be a better place. So far, there was just one place: my life, my brain, the things I had done.

I still thought about telling someone. That was

more of a daydream now, a fantasy—it wasn't something I seriously considered, not in the real world. Part of the problem was momentum. It was hard to stop a lie once it got going. Also, layers of other things built up over time. Secrets had a way of getting buried under the everyday routines of life. And once they were deep underground, they were harder to dig up, and what would be the point anyway?

One thing was for sure: I was never going to forget. Maybe it was true that time healed all wounds, but it couldn't erase the scars. Twenty years from now, I would not look back on my high-school days with fond memories of girls and parties and football games. My clearest memory would be that security guard on those tracks. And it always would be.

I was also never going to feel the same about the people in my life. I would still have "friends," but not like a normal person. That really was the worst part: not ever feeling quite right around other people. Not ever being able to truly relax and just laugh and be honest. I didn't know what to do about that. I didn't know if that would change.

I noticed that I'd started talking to myself. Not every once in a while, like a normal person, but all the time. I carried on whole conversations while I sat alone on the bus or drove my mom's car. I don't know who I was talking to: Detective Brady, my friends, God. Sometimes I would explain things, try to justify myself; I would hold a little press conference in my head. *The thing people don't understand about my situation . . .*

Other times I would talk about stupid stuff, like: *I think I'll make a ham sandwich when I get home, and watch* The Daily Show.

I guess it made me feel better. Maybe it was a form of prayer; maybe all my mutterings were really one long conversation with God. Which sounds profound and "spiritual" and all that, but to be honest, I would rather have talked to a real person.

But that was exactly what I couldn't do.

Thanksgiving came and went and then one day Jared and Paul Auster came to my locker. I hadn't talked to them in a while, but they made a special point to invite me to come skate with them after school at City Hall. It was cold and dry and sunny that day and I said yeah.

We drove there in Paul's car after school. I sat in the back. At one point, Jared leaned over the seat and told me how a bunch of them had been talking about me, and they were worried about me, with my parents getting divorced and all, and why didn't I skate with them more? "Skating's the best cure for parent problems," said Paul.

It was pretty cool they said that. Jared and Paul were not the kind of guys who talked about family stuff. Neither was I. But it was nice.

Christian Barlow met us at City Hall. A bunch of different skaters were there. Everyone was trying to ride the low rail along this handicapped walkway. This cool Hawaiian guy rode it the whole way and almost landed it. His friend videotaped him. Everyone else was falling and crashing pretty bad.

I couldn't do it, but I practiced other stuff with another guy who showed me how to get higher on my ollies. I felt a sense of relief, just being there. I liked hanging out with Christian Barlow and especially Paul, who was pretty hilarious when he talked about girls and stuff that went on at school.

Then someone decided to go to Paranoid Park. I think the Hawaiian guy was going there with his friends, so Paul wanted to go, too. Christian and Jared were all for it. I guess no one was thinking about what happened in September anymore, since it was December. They just said, "Let's go to Paranoid!" and everyone jumped in their various cars.

I was less enthusiastic about Paranoid, needless to say. My stomach tightened into knots as we crossed the bridge. We circled underneath and drove into the industrial area. It was late afternoon, almost dark; the tops of the old warehouse buildings were catching the last of the sunlight. Everything else was dark and shadowy.

As we parked, a blue sedan drove by. It looked like Detective Brady's car. I tried to see inside it, but I couldn't make out who was driving. Also, I didn't want the other guys to see me staring. So I sat back.

That would be my strategy for my return to Paranoid. Just lay back. Keep my mouth shut. Stay out of trouble.

We parked and grabbed our boards and climbed up the dirt embankment. On the cement platform, we stood for a moment and checked out the park. It looked different from how I remembered. It looked cleaner somehow, smaller, not as threatening. The floodlights were on; the heat of them warmed the cement and made everything seem safe and okay.

The other guys didn't hesitate. Christian dropped into the main bowl. Paul and Jared were right behind him. Christian tried to grind the lip and fell and almost hit Paul. But everyone was psyched. Everyone was into it.

I dropped in and worked my way around. I was careful, though, scanning the dozen or so people for anyone I remembered, checking the parking lot on the opposite end for any familiar faces. I didn't see anyone. It seemed pretty safe. Besides us and the Hawaiian crew, it was a pretty quiet night at Paranoid.

I started to relax. I tried a lip-grind and almost got it. An hour went by, and I forgot my problems. I began to enjoy myself, and I realized how much I loved Paranoid. I wondered if I should have come back earlier. Maybe all I needed was to face my fears.

That's when I looked over my shoulder and saw a group of people arriving in the lower parking lot. They were Streeters, guys mostly, with boards and forties of Olde English 800. There were two girls, too. One of them looked familiar. One of them was Paisley.

I didn't panic. I worked my way around to the far bowl and popped out and stood behind two other guys standing along the lip. I watched the Streeters file into the park. I watched Paisley. She looked different in winter clothes. She wore a big newsboy hat. But her hair was the same, dyed black, and her face still had that stone-age look to it—that pale, wasted look. She stopped by the big cement wall and talked to the other girl. I did my best to blend into the scenery.

It didn't work. She saw me. I don't know how; she

wasn't even looking around. But suddenly she stared straight at me. A look of shock and surprise came over her face.

I turned away. I was wearing a wool hat, which I now pulled closer down around my face. But it was too little, too late.

Paisley said something to her friend and began walking in my direction. None of her friends seemed to notice what she was doing. Still, it was not a good situation. As she got closer, it became very clear she had something to say to me. I could feel my heart pounding in my throat as she approached. When she got close, I kinda smiled and nodded to her.

She didn't nod back. "What are you doing here?" she hissed.

"Nothin'. Hangin' out."

"You better leave. Scratch's friends are here."

"So?"

"So, they'll see you!"

I looked passed her at her friends. "But I didn't do anything."

"Are you kidding me? Scratch had to leave town. They almost caught him. Why are you even here?"

"But it was an accident."

"Not according to those guys. They think you did it, and they blame you for all the police coming around."

I hadn't seen any police around. Except for that blue car when we first pulled in.

Behind Paisley, I could see a second group of Streeters coming up from the parking lot. There were six or seven of them. Paisley saw them, too. "You better be careful," she whispered. "You shouldn't even be here."

With that, she turned and walked quickly back to her friend. I turned my back so the others wouldn't see my face.

I still wasn't clear what the Streeters had against me. Or why it was my fault. Shouldn't they respect me for standing up to a security guard?

I decided to bail anyway. Why push my luck? I'd think of some excuse to tell Jared later. I stuck my iPod buds in my ears and casually ambled toward the dirt embankment. Without looking back, I dropped onto the dirt path and crawled through the fence. I slid and skidded down the embankment to the bottom. I dropped my board and started skating. I thought I'd made a pretty smooth escape, but when I looked back, someone was standing at the fence. He seemed to be watching me.

Then he pointed at me and shouted something to his friends.

I could feel the panic rising inside me as I pushed down the road. I turned right and coasted through the main industrial area. Some bums were drinking beer on one of the loading docks. I pushed harder, got past them, and turned left behind the big United Textile building. I checked behind me at every turn. At the train tracks, I hopped off my board and ran across the gravel. I didn't know where I was going, or why exactly I was running.

But I *was* running. I couldn't stop myself. My heart pounded violently in my chest. I was scared to death. Still. After two and a half months. I was so scared every joint in my body shook. All this tension and fear, it had been inside me all this time, and I hadn't even noticed.

I skated across the big parking lot toward the river. It was the same parking lot I had fled across on September seventeenth. Above me was the same cold sky that had haunted me since that night. That deep, black, crushing sky . . .

━◆━◆━◆━◆━◆━◆━◆━◆━◆━━

I was at the far end of the parking lot when they appeared. They came from the right. It was totally dark now, and I heard them first—that low rumble of wheels on pavement. Then I saw them: four guys—four

Streeters—all on boards, all pushing hard and gaining on me.

"Hey, kid!" one shouted, an evil grin on his face. "Where ya goin'?"

The others grinned as well. This wasn't just about defending Scratch's honor; it was also a golden opportunity to beat the crap out of a defenseless Prep.

They were pushing as hard as they could. I pushed hard, too.

"Hey! What are you running for?!" yelled a different one. "We just wanna talk!"

There was an incline now, in the direction of the river. I pushed as hard as I could and went into a low crouch for maximum speed. They did the same. They were getting closer. I waited until they were a few feet behind me, then swung hard to the right, cutting across the nose of the closest guy. He lost his balance and fell on his ass. I stayed in my crouch and aimed for the thick brush along the side of the parking lot. I had gained some ground. If I could get to the brush I could lose them, I could hide. I felt like I had a chance.

But then I saw the fence, chain-link, between me and the brush. Where did that come from? I veered to the left. At that moment, the next closest guy got to me. He grabbed at me and we bumped into each other. By some miracle he lost his speed and I didn't.

But the others closed in. Another guy pulled even with me, about five feet to my right. "Hey, kid!" he hissed. "We got something for you! From Scratch!"

I swerved straight at him and kicked my board at his ankles. He tripped and fell; and I sprinted for the brush. I ran so fast my legs barely stayed under me. I jumped for the fence and scrambled up the chain-link.

I didn't make it. One hand grabbed my leg, another got my ankle. A third found the back of my pants. The weight of the three of them ripped me off the fence. I landed hard, on my side, on the cement.

For a moment I lay stunned. I think someone spit on me. "Way to go, Prep!" said a voice. "Way to sell out to the cops!"

I tried to roll over. "But I didn't!" I groaned. "I swear I didn't say any—!"

Someone kicked me hard in the side, knocking the wind out of me. "Whud you say, Prep? What was that?"

"I *swear*—" I croaked.

Another kick in the back. I tried to roll away from them. I tried to cover my head. All I could think was: *I am so dead. I am so, so dead.*

Then a siren squawked. A bright light flashed across the fence, illuminating the group of us. It was a police car, driving very fast, headed right toward us. It skidded to a stop, and my attackers scattered in every direction.

I could hear the footsteps running away. Slowly, carefully, I unrolled myself and lifted my head. I was staring into the headlights of an unmarked police car; the red police light turned circles from the dash. I looked to my right and saw two plainclothes cops chasing the Streeters.

One of the cops stopped at the end of the fence and jogged back to see if I was okay. I was still in the headlights so I couldn't see who it was at first. But the voice was familiar. So were the thick hands that helped me up: It was Detective Brady.

Of course it was.

─·─·─·─·─·─·─·─·─·─·─·─·─·─

Brady didn't say anything. He helped me up and got me inside his car. Then he jumped into the driver's seat and we tore off.

We picked up the other cop. Brady whipped the car around and floored the accelerator. He wanted to head off the Streeters. His partner called other squad cars to help, referring to the "suspects." In my muddled brain, I tried to figure out what had happened. Did he think the Streeters had committed the train-yard murder? Or was he after them for beating me up? Or was he after them because they were Streeters, and were always the natural suspects in any situation?

Brady couldn't find them. His partner barked at the other cars on his radio. One of them, a normal police car, came rocketing around a corner and almost hit us. Detective Brady cursed him out.

Then a different squad car reported four young men running toward the River Walk. Brady spun his car around and drove there, screeching into the River Walk parking lot and skidding to a stop. He and his partner jumped out and ran down the grass hill.

I got out of the car, too, but Brady waved for me to stay put.

So I did. I stood next to the unmarked police car and watched Brady and his partner jog across the grass in the moonlight.

A moment later, another cop car pulled in beside Brady's car. These policemen, in uniforms, walked quickly in the same direction. They all disappeared under the Morrison Bridge.

At this point, I looked down at my hands and saw

they were dirty and cut up from getting jerked off the fence. The Streeters had me. They had me dead. If Brady hadn't come along, who knows what would have happened.

I felt a deep shiver pass through me then. My whole body began to shake. I crawled into the passenger seat of Detective Brady's warm car. It was the same car I had ridden in before, which made me feel better. A strange calmness came over me. I had the thought: *I could tell Brady the truth.*

I stared at the river and the city beyond it. Detective Brady was the key. He was the person I had been looking for, the person I could trust, the person who understood. He'd been right in front of me all this time. Why hadn't I seen that?

My eyes teared up. I began to cry. I felt all the tension that I had been holding in my body finally begin to melt and let go. I wiped the tears off my face with my shirtsleeve. I found some old Dunkin' Donuts napkins on the seat and blew my nose.

As I dabbed my eyes and face, I spotted something else on the seat. It was a greeting card, in an envelope. I was sitting on it, crushing it. I scooted to the side and pulled it out. The return address caught my eye. It said "Mr. and Mrs. Edwin Brady."

I looked at it while I blew my nose again. Who was

Edwin Brady? It had to be a relative. It couldn't be his parents; his parents were divorced.

But now I was curious. I held the envelope in the moonlight. It was addressed to Matthew Brady, and it was from Mr. and Mrs. Edwin Brady. I pulled the card out. On the cover was a picture of a scenic mountaintop. The inside was blank, but with this handwritten note:

> *Dear Matthew and Lisa,*
>
> *Thank you so much for helping us celebrate our fortieth wedding anniversary. May your years together be as happy and joyous as ours have been.*
>
> *Love, Mom and Dad*

I tried to think how this could be. Detective Brady's parents were divorced. He had told me that himself, when I told him about my own family.

Had he meant *he* was divorced? But he obviously wasn't. He was married to this Lisa person.

I sat in the car and read the card again. I looked at the envelope. Detectives couldn't lie to you, could they? Wasn't that illegal? Like, a cop could say something to scare you, but a detective, trying to solve a case, can't just flat-out *lie* to you. That wouldn't be right. They would get in trouble. Even if it was something that had nothing to do with the case, right? They couldn't just make stuff up, to trick you, to make you like them or trust them or whatever. . . .

Could they?

⊷⊷⊷⊷⊷⊷⊷⊷⊷⊷⊷⊷⊷⊷⊷⊷

The night air seemed colder when I got out of Brady's car. I pulled my track jacket closer around me as I shut the door. One of the cops turned when he heard it slam. But he didn't say anything. He didn't try to stop me.

I walked across the parking lot, away from the river. Another police car was parked at the other end. I couldn't see if anyone was in it.

I kept walking, across Grand Avenue, under the highway, back to the access road. I walked across the silent, deserted parking lot and found my board lying upside down next to the chain-link fence. The Streeters' boards were there, too, scattered here and there. I left them and walked north to MLK Boulevard, to where the buses ran.

I'm not sure what I was thinking as I did this. I had a strange conviction that nothing would happen to me. Not that night. And I was right. No one came after me. No one chased me down.

At MLK, the 57 bus had just pulled in. I hopped on. I was still shaking slightly as I walked down the aisle. I took the fourth seat from the back, the same one I sat in with Macy that night on Vista. That was going to be *my seat* from now on, I decided.

The bus left a moment later. It drove over the river and up Burnside toward the West Side. I watched cars pass by out the window. I watched houses nestled in the trees along the road. I didn't talk to myself that night. I just sat there. My brain was a blank. I didn't think about anything.

At my neighborhood stop, I got off the bus and walked down my street. I hoped I wouldn't have to deal with anyone at home, and I got my wish. My mom was sprawled on the couch, snoring in front of the TV. Henry was asleep, too, in the big chair. I walked through to the stairs and went up to my room. I took off my clothes and took a shower.

Back in my room, I put on clean underwear, a clean T-shirt. I turned on my radio and listened to the end of that night's Trail Blazers game. As I crawled into bed, I felt that familiar ache in my chest, that fear of being caught, or found out or whatever. But I didn't let it bother me. None of this was my fault. I was just some kid. I lay down and pulled the covers up to my neck. I blinked at the ceiling. *God, you put me in this place*, I said. *You can't blame me for trying to survive.*

Then I rolled over, and in a few short minutes I was asleep.

During the next couple days, I felt my usual anxieties: waiting for the phone to ring, for Brady to show up, for the regular police to pull me out of class and lead me away in handcuffs.

They never did. Nothing happened. No one came.

The divorce stuff continued. Unlike murders, every detail of the divorce was studied and discussed by a vast array of experts. One Saturday, a male friend of my mom who was a divorce lawyer came over and tried to help her. He spread out a bunch of papers on the kitchen table, and they drank coffee and talked all afternoon.

I stayed away from the kitchen during that. I went out to the driveway to practice my ollies. I set up a line of empty pop cans and practiced jumping over them. After a couple passes I fell on my ass. I rolled onto my back and just lay there for a minute, in the middle of my driveway. It was weird lying on the cold cement, staring up at the gray winter sky. It was kinda cool. The sky looked so big and open and almost *friendly*. It made me feel good to stare into it. The blankness. The emptiness.

"Hello?" said a voice.

I lifted my head. It was Macy. I put my head back down and closed my eyes.

"Hel-*lo*?" she repeated. "Why are you lying in the middle of your driveway?"

"Because."

"Are you dead?"

"Do I look dead?"

"A little."

She was on a bike. It must have been her dad's; it was too big for her, and she had to put her foot on the curb to not fall over.

I stood up then. I picked up my board. I rode down the driveway into the street and grabbed the back of her bike.

"What are you doing?" she asked.

"Pull me."

"I can't."

"Sure you can. Pedal!" I pushed her bike forward and she had no choice but to pedal.

"I can't—"

"Go!"

I pushed her. We got a little speed going. She started to tow me. We went halfway down the block. Then we went back the other way.

After that, we sat on the curb at the end of the block.

I sat on my board. She chewed a piece of gum.

"So I was thinking," she said, blowing a bubble and then pulling it into a long string.

"What about?"

"Like, what you were saying. Like, if you did something that you couldn't tell anyone."

I didn't want to talk about that now. "It doesn't matter. Forget it."

"What I would do is . . ." she said. "I would write a letter."

"Yeah?" I said. "To who?"

"To the person you did it to. Like an apology or whatever."

I didn't answer.

"Or maybe to someone else," she said. "Maybe a separate person, someone you feel comfortable with. But the point is to tell it and get it off your chest. All the details, all the things you've been obsessing about. Get it all out on paper."

"And then what?"

"Then you'll feel better."

"Yeah?" I asked. "And what do I do with the letter?"

"Whatever you want," she said, stuffing the gum back into her mouth. "Save it. Burn it. Send it to the person. It doesn't really matter. Writing it down, that's the important thing. This psychologist made me do that when I was having a big fight with my mom."

"I don't know. It sounds like a homework assignment."

"Trust me, once you get going, it's not like a homework assignment. It feels so good to say all the stuff you're thinking. It's a big relief."

"Yeah, maybe."

"The trick is," she said, "write it to someone you can really talk to. You know? Like, write it to someone that you feel comfortable with. Like, not a teacher or your parents or whatever. Write it to a friend."

"Yeah . . ." I said.

"Write it to me," she said, her voice softening slightly.

I thought about that. Then her cell phone rang. She stood up and answered it. It was her mom. She walked across the street as they argued.

I sat on my skateboard and squinted into the sky.

Dear _____,

So I guess that's what these are. My letters to you, Macy McLaughlin. Or that's what they turned into. You sort of are the person I feel "most comfortable with," so I guess it makes sense.

You were so right, though. Every page I've written has felt like a weight off my shoulders. When you really get going, writing is like talking to your best friend, except they can't interrupt you or tell you what an idiot you are.

Anyway . . . what else can I tell you before I finish this? The ocean's pretty quiet tonight. (It's almost midnight now.) My uncle Tommy is downstairs cooking something. It was nice of him to invite me to come to his beach house for winter break. He's been super cool about everything. He's worried about me, I guess; he acts like I'm this fragile person now, with the divorce going on. He never pries or asks me what I do up here all night, scribbling away like some crazy person or whatever.

⇥⇥⇥⇥⇥⇥⇥⇥⇥⇥⇥⇥⇥⇥⇥

So anyway, the main thing I wanted to say to you before I end this is: thank you. I'm not sure for what, exactly. For being there, I guess. For riding the bus with me up Vista that night. And for occupying my brain. I sort of think about you now. Mostly because I've been writing you these endless letters. But at other times, too, like walking on the beach, or at night before I fall asleep. I always wondered what would replace those horrible pictures in my head. I never thought it would be the annoying sixth-grader who lived down the street.

As for what I'll do . . . who knows? I still have days when I expect Brady to show up at my door with hand-cuffs. Other times, I want to walk into a police station myself and confess everything. I wish I trusted people more. I wish I had more faith in things. On the other hand, why tempt fate? It's not like adults always do the right thing. They're more screwed up than teenagers. At least we know how full of crap we are.

That's the thing about hanging out with you these last couple months. You kinda saved my ass. The reason is: I trust you. I really do. And that's all it takes.

Knowing there's one person out there on your side, one person who's got your back. That's enough to keep you sane.

Oh, yeah, and since I know this is the end, I guess I can say one other thing: I sort of like you. I know. Isn't that ridiculous? And so typical. The minute you stop liking me, I start liking you. God messes with you that way. He totally does. It's all part of the great cosmic joke.

Okay, Macy McLaughlin. It's late now and I'm gonna stop. Thanks for keeping me company. Thanks for a lot of things.

Now I'm going to go find some matches. . . .